Hakra

A Story

By

C. Schmidt

HAKRA

SLEEK PUBLISHING GROUP | MARYLAND

Contact: C. Schmidt Email: scholarman@gmail.com

Phone: 301-842-4326 **Website**: www.scholarman.com

Instagram/Twitter: @ScholarMan **Facebook**: ScholarMan Music

ISBN: 978-0-578-89116-3

Cover design by: Local Summer CO | www.localsummerco.com

About C. Schmidt: C. Schmidt is Maryland-based hip-hop artist and producer, who is originally from Alexandria, Virginia. He found a new passion for creative writing after being featured as a contributing author on a hip-hop music blog. He found a new use for his pen, after providing several music reviews, articles and essays. A new flame for connecting words ignited inside of him. Sharing stories became one of his greatest desires in this world, whether it be through the written or spoken word.

He continues to produce and release music independently - under the pseudonym ScholarMan - when he is not writing. He has numerous albums available online. During his downtime, he loves spending time with his daughter, exercising, and playing poker, shooting pool, and watching movies. His favorite genres are horror, sci-fi thrillers and comedies.

HAKRA

Miss you, momma. - C.

PROLOGUE

Some time ago, a major event abruptly changed everyone's lives in a metropolis called Pineville. A large, strange object fell from the sky, cracking the land within Pineville. Over time, it physically divided and changed it. The event, which further created a mixture of confusion, fear, and intrigue; gradually brought about changes within everyone's genetics. Even though it caused some people to become better citizens, others became worse. They became horrible versions of themselves; monstrous.

Many of the good banded together, doing their best to rebuild from their losses. The Guardian, among the first of those people, put forth efforts that led to the creation of Hock City. Later, Uhmandra was created. But there were some others who used the event to gradually gain power. Secretly they used the event to position themselves to control others. Now more divided than ever, Pineville has been separated into regions due to the event. While some are friendly, others are not so much.

Through his journeys, Langston came across some of these types of people. He has made new friends and allies, shaking up their once quiet lives. But everything he and friends think they know about the event . . . will change once they meet Hakra.

HAKRA

Chapter 1

HOCK CITY - THE EARLY DAYS

BEFORE THE HUMAN FROM UHMANDRA ARRIVED AT HOCK City's walls - before the city became a mixing bowl of perilous creatures, greed, and violence - the original Guardian spent countless time in his basement, studying and planning. While seated at a large roundtable, he reflected and wrote out his thoughts.

On one of these occasions, his documents were scattered about, altogether covering the table. These documents were filled with his theories. Sometimes, the writing lined every inch of the paper. Often times, he had written so much that some of the writing was illegible to anyone but himself. But mostly, he wrote quickly, since his thoughts moved faster than his hand could keep up.

While writing, he mostly drank aged wine from his private collection. He gradually began building the collection, even before the events that changed everything. This collection started with twelve bottles, all acquired from a sixty-dollar-a-month wine club. His wife had joined the club some time before the obscure object was first seen in the sky.

The Ms. had managed to save up to seventy-eight bottles rather quickly. In part, the club gave her double the number of bottles during the first month. She received a few for free after becoming a new member. She was so excited about this that she didn't want to drink some of the wine too soon.

She took a liking to collecting the wines, calling the membership a hobby; one in which The Guardian had initially cringed. But as time moved on, he didn't mind. At first, he wondered daily where he was going to store the collection.

Before the events, he and his wife lived in their humble home in Pineville where they often cooked together. Each drank from one of the bottles until they were too tipsy to eat. So, they would let the food simmer. They would first have dessert while the kids were busying themselves. Then, they would return to eating the food in the wee hours of the morning.

After the event and after several cycles had passed, the Guardian would eventually combine what he had left of these bottles - a total in which he lost count. Then, he put similar wines into large barrels. He would let them go through the cellaring process, at which he was an amateur. Still, he learned enough about it through his research and talking with other wine aficionados. Around this time, he only had a few barrels lined against one of the basement walls in the mansion.

To avoid consuming the wine too quickly, he would drink other alcoholic beverages that his team of barters managed to gather during various trips into Pineville. He grew a liking to ale, a combination of beer and moonshine that his elders bottled and drank throughout his young adulthood.

It was also hard for him to drink the wine, however, since he thought of his now deceased wife with each barrel he stored. He even had a little message handwritten on each bottle: For my love. Though, on this day, he drank willingly as he wrote. His thoughts must have been heavy.

They demanded a taste of the strong, tasty beverage to ease the weight.

For a moment, the only sounds in the basement were the pen moving across paper, the echo from deep gulps of wine, and - every now and then - a sigh or a cough. There were also subtle noises of various species of insects and small mammals moving around the room. These rodents found their way into the home through small openings as most do, but some were . . . special. Also filling the space at times were the sounds of footsteps traveling from upstairs. The mansion staff constantly moved back and forth, from the kitchen to various rooms, as they cooked and cleaned.

The mansion was much smaller at this time. So, almost every sound by the individuals in the home could be heard by others nearby, especially The Guardian. One of his new abilities was improved hearing.

Some of the footsteps grew heavier. They seemed to travel toward the main floor's basement entrance, making their way slowly down the stairs. Having almost learned the difference in the footsteps of the mansion's regulars, The Guardian could tell a visitor was approaching.

These particular footsteps were rapid and light. The person connected to the footsteps sucked their teeth quietly, before sighing. Clearly annoyed by something.

Almost immediately, The Guardian recognized the sound and knew who approached.

"Growing tired of your visits, brother?" The Guardian says with a chuckle. He doesn't turn his attention away from his papers, but continues to write with the sound of the pen moving across the paper that grows a bit louder. "Or are you getting out of shape, old man?"

"Oh shut up!" Winston replies, adjusting his attire. He was fond of his clothing. Most of the time, he wore three-piece suits and dress shoes.

The Guardian smiled to himself at his brother's response.

"Come now. I will never grow tired of visiting this *lovely* place of yours," Winston continues, sarcastically. "But you have a perfectly good office on the main floor. Why do you choose to spend your time in this cold, filthy basement?" He approaches the roundtable.

"This is my place of peace. I like it down here."

Winston scoffs. "You enjoy the critters, too?" He points to a nearby wall where a small audience of rodents seem to watch them, listening to the conversation.

The Guardian laughs. "They don't bother me. So why do they bother you?"

Winston waves his hand, disregarding his brother's question.

"Sit, brother. What brings you here?"

"Figured I would stop by . . . I don't need anything specific."

Nodding slowly, The Guardian takes a moment to reply. "I wish you would move here with us. You have been spending a lot of time back in our old neighborhood. I'm sure these good people would build for you, as they have done for me. After all, you are my brother and have been a great help, of course."

Sighing, Winston says, "This city – this place . . . is your thing. I am just helping you when I can. Besides . . . I like our old neighborhood. I love my home. I love our old neighborhood."

The Guardian chuckles, grabbing his cup of ale and throwing back a long portion of the potent beverage. He grabbed another cup and poured some for Winston, sliding it across the table.

"What are you writing now? Let me guess –" Winston interrupts his own comments, taking a sip of the ale.

"Yes, yes, Winston. I am still working."

"You are going to kill yourself obsessing over this," Winston reclines back in his chair, putting his feet on the table.

"Someone needs to obsess over it."

Winston sucks his teeth.

A brief moment of silence overcomes the room. The two continue sipping their drinks, as a cold breeze enters the room. It shifts some papers from the various stacks. The Guardian continues to write while Winston browses through some of the papers on the table.

"Anything new to report with your abilities?" The Guardian asks.

"No. Not really. Other than trying to keep the thoughts of others out of my own. It can be a mess upstairs, you know. Have you been practicing control over yours?"

"I haven't any choice. If I didn't, I would destroy everything I touch. But it's a challenge. If I don't have control over my own abilities and behavior, what kind of leader would I be?"

"Yes, but you know just as well as I do that many of us are still getting used to our abilities – after all this time."

"Indeed." The Guardian reclines back in his chair and gazes at the ceiling. "These people – they have gotten too comfortable with the changes," he says.

"So?"

"So, you know just as well as I do that, in the beginning of all this, almost all of us wanted to figure out what was happening. Many of us wanted to know what was changing us. Now . . . now it seems like people are slowly starting to give up."

"Or could it be they are just accepting things for what they are? Adapting maybe?" Winston replies.

The Guardian doesn't respond at first. Instead, he sighs before sitting upright and shuffles some papers. He paused and stared at one of the barrels of wine. "Some, yes. But I believe that's because no one is talking about it anymore. We have to do more than just control our abilities. We need to dig deeper into what happened that night. We must discover what changed us all, before that thing completely destroys everything we knew and loved."

"Hmm. I'm with you, brother. But this is no easy task to do." Winston strokes his striking, black beard. He carefully watches the demeanor of The Guardian. "Well, no matter what – I got your back. I just don't want you to stress yourself to death over this."

"Have you seen Franklin or Shaida?"

Winston chuckled. "Those children of yours have become very active since you moved them into this city. More than what they were out yonder. They seem to love what you created here."

"I wish you would stop saying that."

"What? You did create this place, didn't you?" Winston chuckles.

"These people needed someone to follow, and for some reason, they chose me."

Looking away briefly, Winston replies, "You don't seem to have a problem with it."

"Someone needed to step up. Otherwise, the land we have come to call home would be much worse."

Winston reared back in his chair and folded his arms. "Where is Kinth? I already know where Shaida is. She's following behind Franklin's nonsense, I'm sure."

"Not sure exactly. I asked him to travel some into the Pines. He's working with others to expand and acquire resources."

"Should I schedule the next council meeting?" Winston lets his chair drop abruptly.

"Yes, but not yet."

Curiously, Winston replies, "Not yet?"

"I want to present more ideas for my plans at the next meeting. But I need more time," The Guardian replies emphatically.

"About that . . . you know some of the council doesn't agree with you regarding this."

"*Some* or someone?"

The two share a brief, deep stare.

Chapter 2

HOCK CITY & THE PINES - PRESENT DAY

PRESENTLY, AN EERIE SILENCE HAS FALLEN ACROSS HOCK city, making its way outside of the gates and into the Pines. The once busy, crowded streets inside of the walls have been converted to the equivalent of a large library, with the remaining people inside whispering to one another about the recent events. Others have hidden in various areas, hoping that the city's security didn't find them.

All the lights at Madam Pearl's place have gone dark, like many of the other buildings nearby. Security has positioned themselves at all entrances and exits, ensuring that any remaining people are captured. But the Line District is desolate, having been almost completely evacuated due to The Guardian's recent orders. A big difference from the hundreds of people who would normally be moving along the streets.

The streets are full of debris. It glides across the ground from the wind; with not a soul in sight except for a few. The Mantis walks alone, his arms crossed behind his back. He looks at what was left of the city of which he had been so fond since the human came. He is evidently troubled, looking almost exacerbated – as much as his triangular face would allow.

Behind him in the distance, a group of armed guards follow. They wonder about their next orders, because the Mantis has not said anything to them yet. The quiet is becoming uncomfortable. Constantly, they look at each other and their surroundings and patiently wait for further instructions.

The Mantis pauses his stride, picking up one of the papers that blew across the ground and over his feet. They had made its way to being wrapped around a pole. The paper is one of many flyers distributed by The Guardian, regularly promoting his new leadership since he stole the reins from his father: YOU ARE SAFE HERE. YOUR ABILITIES ARE YOUR OWN. EVERYONE IS WELCOME AT HOCK CITY.

The citizens of this city have been forced beyond the walls. Now, they must fend for themselves in unfamiliar areas. They flocked to any nearby dwelling, hoping to get their families inside before the next cycle of darkness came – hoping to regroup. Hunger and thirst are the only things resting on their minds.

The sky has also oddly changed, and many have taken notice. Adding to the fear, the changes in the sky begin to affect the locals' already nervous demeanors. Some began to lash out toward others; people they had known for many cycles. It was as if something was controlling their behavior.

Beginning to fight, some throw random objects in an attempt to harm each other. They use their abilities against anyone who intervenes their attempts to find basic resources to survive. Many set fires and caused other distractions, with the hopes of getting away with any goods they could manage.

A random family consisting of a mother and two teenage boys find themselves near the commotion. The mother does her best to shield her sons by keeping close to the shadows and dark sides of buildings. All remain unseen. She buys time by draping a large, dark-colored blanket over her boys in order to disguise them, blending them with the color of the buildings.

Out of breath, she kneels to one knee and watches the rioting, contemplating the next thing to do.

"Mother," the eldest of the two boys says. "We need to get away from here. Those people from inside the walls. I have never seen them act like this before."

"They're scary," the younger brother adds, pulling the blanket down a bit to cover more of his face. The color of his face flickers.

"Shh. I know." The mother studies the area. "Follow me and keep quiet. Do not . . . do *not* use your gifts. Do you understand?"

The boys shake their heads nervously, as they formed a single line, following behind their mother closely. She weaves them between some of the homes, garbled cars, and piles of debris. She does the best she can to move unnoticed. Accidentally she kicks a plastic bottle, causing it to roll across the ground.

A random, local man notices the three of them and confronts the group without saying anything. He looks over the mother first in a creepy fashion, as if he was studying her. Preparing an evil deed within his mind, he rubs his hands together and forms a threatening smile.

Before he can speak, the mother quickly immobilizes him; punching him brutally in the throat. Grabbing at his neck, the man struggles to breathe while falling to his knees. The mother then kicked him in the face, delivering a hard enough blow to knock him out cold. Quickly, she dragged him across the ground. She hides his body behind an old dumpster.

"C'mon," she whispers to her sons. "We need to move faster."

The three continued their short journey through the chaos, making their way to a slightly more barren area of homes. As they grew closer to this area, the noise of the rioting fades.

"Mom, I'm tired," the younger of the two boys says, slowing his pace.

The mother, smiling slightly, rubbed the boy's head and face affectionately. Looking back, she frowns at the chaos still happening behind them. Snapping out of her gaze, she continues to walk in the opposite direction and inspects the new area of tightly spaced homes. Some are cramped and others connect to form small buildings.

Quickly, she picks a home that seemed safe, completing a quick run around it to ensure it was empty. At each grubby window, she peaks inside and listens for any odd sounds. She notices that the other homes nearby were just as dark and quiet. After exhaling deeply, she instructs the boys to run inside, using only a hand gesture.

The boys walk quietly through the small foyer, doing their best to keep quiet. With the exception of one of the doors creaking, they were off to a good start. Walking down the hall, they briefly peak at the kitchen. There, they notice plates of food that seemed to be half-eaten. The mother follows, looking beyond them as they walked. She snaps her fingers once to get their attention. Quietly, she directs them to what appeared to be one of two bedrooms.

As they enter the bedroom, the oldest of the brothers stopped abruptly. He notices that the room appeared to have been ransacked. Across the hall, the mother notices a similar mess in the adjacent room. She takes a closer look at the area as her sons did the same.

"Looks like someone used to live here . . . like *really* recently," the older brother whispers. "It still feels warm in here."

"Yeah," the younger brother responds, placing his hand on the wall to rub his fingers across old, peeling stickers. "Was this a kid's room?"

"Looks that way," the mother said, sitting down on an old bean bag near a wall. "Get some rest," she adds as she rested hear head against the wall and closes her eyes. The two boys laid down side by side on the bed, staring at the ceiling.

Not long after the three settled in, sounds of a distant conversation and footsteps awaken the mother. Standing slowly, she listens for a moment before taking steps to a nearby window. Looking at her boys first, who are sound asleep, she listens to the footsteps and conversation that seemed to be growing louder. In the corner of the room near the window was a plastic bin that was halfway full of various toys. Anxiously she grabs a toy gun and puts it in her waist band.

The conversation between the people continues just outside the window.

"I'm just saying, Jack. I don't know why you brought that old man to our area," a man with a husky voice says. "You put us all at risk!"

"I didn't bring anybody, anywhere. He just showed up," Jack responds, stopping briefly. "What was I supposed to do? Just send him away?"

"Well, you didn't have to be so nice. You know as well as I do that we can't trust nobody out here."

Growing frustrated, Jack shakes his head. "Will you shut up?! Just for a minute. Shut the hell up. I've been out here just as long as you. I know most people can't be trusted. But something felt different about him. I just wanted to know if he knew anything that might help us. Don't you want to find out what's going on?"

The other man scoffs.

"Let's just check on Eli and then get back," Jack adds.

Still listening, the mother realizes that the group of people were getting closer to the front door of the home in which she and her boys were squatting. She tries to quickly grab her things, shaking the boys to wake up. But then, someone knocks on the front door.

"Hey, Eli!" Jack says in a loud whisper. He stepped back a few steps from the door. "Eli! We just wanted to see if you are okay. We heard about what happened at the Exchange."

The man's words are met with silence. Repeating himself, he is surprised at the response.

"There ain't no Eli here!" the mother yells, standing just to the side of the door.

"Who's that?" one of the men say aloud. He does his best to whisper but failed. "Jack, that don't sound like Eli's wife."

The mother continues to listen, responding when necessary. "Cause I ain't his wife! And there's no Eli here!

I'm just passin' through and needed somewhere to sleep for the night."

"But where is Eli? Can I at least come in?" Jack replies; confused. "We are just friends of his and wanted to see him."

"No! He's not here!"

A heavy silence falls around the home. Jack gazes at the ground and then back at the small group of people who came with him. Most of the men and the few women looked back at him and each other dumbfounded. Jack looked up at the sky and raised his brows at the odd color of it, pacing a bit before saying anything else.

By this time, the boys are now awake and have crept quietly to the front of the house.

"Mom," the oldest says.

"Get our things, and go out the back window. Hide in the brush. I will be right behind you," the mother said quietly.

"Who is that?" the oldest asked. "Are we in danger?"

"No time; go."

Running down the hall to the back bedroom, the boys do their best to not knock anything over or bump into anything, while their mother gazed at the floor to gather her thoughts.

"Look, we just want to see Eli," Jack adds, walking toward the door. "And if he isn't here . . . well, that's just odd. We . . . we would need an explanation." Jack tries to sound as scary as can, but it wasn't in his nature to make threats.

Hesitating, the mother feels the need to prepare for a fight at first. But then, she hastily changes her mind. She quickly throws the toy gun to the floor and ran behind her sons. Practically gliding through the window they left open, she rejoins them a few yards away behind a raggedy fence.

Almost simultaneously, Jack and the others force the door open and storm into the home. He looks around and notices that the house is a mess, as if someone burglarized it. Peaking down the hall, Jack can see the silhouette of people moving outside. "Hey! I just want to talk to you!" He shouts while running toward the room. Some of the others entered the house to get a better look at what was happening.

Just as Jack gets to the window, he could see three people running away from the home. "I don't know who that was, but it definitely wasn't Eli or his family," he says, leaning with his face almost out of the window.

"Damn, what happened here? Did they rob the place?" another from the group says, looking around.

"Something tells me that woman wasn't lying. With all that shit happening out there, everyone is looking for a safe place to be," Jack adds. "But . . . I don't know."

"What do we do?" the husky-voice man chimes in.

Jack paces around the home, ending up in the kitchen. Running his hands down the cabinet doors as he walks, he opens up a couple of them to see if any food was left. Noticing a plate on the table, he sat down and fingered the food left on it, searching through the bread for a piece that hadn't been touched.

"I think," Jack chews the bread sloppily. "I think Eli left in a hurry. And I don't blame him. We need to get everyone – anyone - together. Need to have a talk. Something is going on, since all those people are suddenly outside the walls. Especially around the same time that Eli was attacked. And especially because of what we already know. That lady represents some bigger happenings."

Jack then abruptly leaves the room before anyone can respond, walking out the front door. The group followed behind him.

Chapter 3

THE PLAN - DELRUSIA ISLAND

ALDO PACES AROUND HIS CELL, AT TIMES HOLDING HIS head close to the gate. He attempts to get a look down the hall. He has become nervous ever since Sir Grace had Kinth removed. Aldo is then taken down several hallways to be placed with the other unknowns.

Seeing his old friend again brought Aldo a new sense of peace and hope. Though he is now disturbed that these feelings have been snatched away, just as fast as they have come. He needs to find a way to connect with Kinth again, but he doesn't know what to do right away. Continuing to pace in a circle, Aldo listens to the various shouting and other odd sounds around him before he stops in his tracks.

Mr. Shush had begun clapping his hands quietly, motioning for Aldo to keep quiet. Creatures with potato sacks were slowly making their way down the corridor, dragging their heavy feet across the stone floor. Letting out a weird squeal, Mr. Shush glows because it was time for chow.

The creature that normally delivered Aldo's sack is back with the goods again. Eyeing Aldo closely, the creature expected the usual sly comment from the prisoner. But Aldo stood perfectly still and returned the same odd gaze. Puzzled by his actions, the creature paused the sack deliveries and approached the gate to Aldo's cell. Squinting his eyes, he tossed a sack on the floor of the cell hesitantly, waiting for Aldo to say something just before grabbing it.

When Aldo doesn't behave as normal, the creature comes even closer to the gate, letting out an aggressive huff. A non-verbal command of sorts, commanding Aldo to grab the steaming hot food and eat. But Aldo doesn't budge. Instead, he stood still. He swayed a little from side to side. Huffing again, the creature pounded on the cell gate. Still nothing.

The creature showed his teeth evilly.

Reaching slowly for the sack, Aldo pulls out as many potatoes that he could hold in one hand. He looks at the potatoes and then at the creature, who was still watching him closely. Without any warning, Aldo throws the potatoes with all his strength toward the creature. The steaming potatoes soar through the air, crashing into the cell gate. They rip apart, leaving chunks of it landing on the creature's face and covering one of its eyes.

Furiously, the creature huffs again. He quickly drops the other sacks of food. Opening the gate, it storms into the cell. Aldo chews one of the potatoes smugly as the creature approaches him. Despite being a bit nervous of his plan, he needed to persevere.

Standing just feet away in front of Aldo, the creature let out a ferocious roar. The roar causes Aldo's cell to shake, along with the others nearby. Bits of gravel bounce across the floor. But Aldo doesn't budge. Instead, he continues to chew the same potato, pausing after a few bites to take a deep breath. The creature, puzzled by Aldo's body language, tilts his head. Smiling, Aldo blows all of the chewed bits of potato on the creature.

Roaring again, the creature rushes Aldo. Grabbing him with both hands, he lifts him into the air and slams him to the floor. The force of the slam knocks Aldo out cold. Leaning in to smell him, the creature grabs him by the legs and drags him down the corridor.

Unaware of what's taking place in another section of the prison, Kinth rested against the wall. He kept a close eye on his father's breathing, which had slowed some. At times, it didn't seem like he wasn't breathing much at all. Thus, the reason why Kinth hadn't slept much. He drifted a couple times but never completely fell asleep.

Because of this and other things, the environment was somber. Many of the others had been watching, noticing Kinth seemed to be in his thoughts, as well as hovering over the well-being of his sickly father. Enrico also kept a close eye, still pondering their discussion about escaping. Even the stranger who had once tried to bully Kinth could be seen observing him. He, too, sensed that something – anything – was going to happen.

A mild glow from the light in the adjacent corridors flickered because of the rapid movement of Sir Grace's creatures. One creature moved more harshly than the others, causing some of the prisoners in the large cell with Kinth to become curious of what was going on. Several of the prisoners began to crowd the cell gate, pressing their faces against the bars to see what they could.

Kinth tilted his head to the side. He could see between the bodies, but he couldn't see much. He was more concerned with his father, watching him and rubbing his brow gently. Gradually he removed himself from under the weight of his father's body and stood to see what the fuss was about.

"What's happening?" he says aloud, to no one in particular.

"They must be bringing a new prisoner down here," a random cellmate replies.

Enrico jumps to his feet as well and approaches. "So what do we do?"

Kinth doesn't respond. Instead, he raises his index finger to his mouth and signals Enrico and others to quiet down. Walking toward the group near the cell gate, he takes a look for himself. Nearby, a creature began to walk violently down the corridor. With one arm behind its back, he smashes his other fist through various blocks of stone. The rumble ran through the walls of the prison like blood through a vein.

"I told you not to hit anything! You are destroying the prison, you brutes!" Sir Grace screams from another section of the prison. "CONTROL YOUR TEMPERS!"

Behind the creature is the faint sound of something dragging across the floor, along with the sound of mumbled words.

This activity's echoes made their way to where Kinth and the others were standing. While the other cellmates were busy shouting at the activity, Kinth strained to get a better listen. *Aldo*, he thought, stepping back from the cell gate and moving against the wall.

The creature forcefully opens the gate, slinging a slightly incoherent Aldo by his legs and into the middle of the cell. Aldo slid across the rough stone floor, bumping into one of the center columns. Nearby prisoners practically jumped on him, searching his clothing for anything they could use. Before they could get far with their search, however, Kinth forcefully broke up the group. He picked up Aldo and brought him near Enrico, who had moved a bit closer to the wall.

Kinth huddled over Aldo, smacking him a few times to awaken him.

"Aldo! Aldo!" Kinth whispers. "Wake up, man! Wake up!"

Enrico lowers to one knee and leaned in as well.

Aldo shifted his head from side to side a little, slightly blinking his eyes. Slowly bringing his hands to his face, he exhaled deeply. "Kinth?"

"Yeah. It's me, brother," Kinth replies. "You alright?"

"I knew it would work." Aldo pushes himself up to a sitting position with Kinth's assistance.

"What's he talkin' about?" Enrico glances over his shoulder, thinking that he was talking too loud.

Aldo takes a quick look over at Enrico. "Who is this guy?" he replies.

"This is Enrico. He's goin' help us get outta here," Kinth says, scanning the cell.

"I knew it! I knew you would get over here and start plotting some shit!" Aldo shouts, moving his arms excitedly.

"Shh. Shh. We're goin' to need everyone's help in here," Kinth replies. "That's the only way this will work."

A small crowd begins to form around the three.

"What's your plan?" Aldo asks.

"How much do we know about this Sir Grace guy?" Kinth strokes his beard.

"He normally walks around twice a day. Even more if there are new prisoners. He should be coming by at any moment now," a random, elderly prisoner chimes in.

"Do you have abilities, old friend?" Kinth asks.

"Yes. But I have been in here for so long that I don't quite remember how to use them."

"Okay. So —" Kinth is interrupted. The shadow of a creature grew on an adjacent wall outside of the cell. Aldo tapped him rapidly, warning him. Once the shadow moved along, Kinth continues. "Okay. Enrico, you and the old man find out who else has abilities. Then, find out who wants to get the fuck outta here. Have these people stand near the gate and against the walls. For everyone else, have them stand against the back wall."

"Then what?"

Kinth gazes at the floor before looking up at all the concerned faces around him. He started to speak but then stopped as he stood to his feet. He looked at them once more. "We hit 'em with everything we got."

"But . . . but it doesn't seem like we got much," Enrico replies fearfully. He mumbles something to himself in his native tongue, sounding worried.

"This guy and I have worked with less. Trust me," Aldo chimes in.

Nodding in agreement, Kinth says, "Just tell everyone with abilities to muster up whatever they have left. When that piece of shit returns, we will attack. We will use

Enrico's ability as a distraction first. Enrico, you know what to do – on my signal."

An intense silence falls among them. Hesitant, Enrico nods before he and the old stranger walk off. They split into twos and speak with the various cellmates.

"What can he do?" Aldo asks.

"Enrico? He has projection abilities. We just need to distract those awful beasts long enough to get everyone out."

"And then what?"

Sighing, Kinth says, "I'm wingin' this one. We do whatever we need to, so that we can get out of here."

Several moments have come and gone, only to be met with silence. The large, shared cell has grown soundless with the exception of random snoring and heavy breathing. The glow of the adjacent hallway lights up a portion of one side of the cell.

Most of the prisoners are no longer at alert, after having waited for some time for Sir Grace to return. Instead, they grew tired and eventually fell asleep. The odd, mysterious overseer of the place has not been back, based on those who knew his normal routine. For those already awake, it seemed as if all eyes were on Kinth.

What happens if Sir Grace never returned?

Kinth is back near his father, who is still resting. This was the longest he had ever seen his father sleep, which was troubling. His breathing was still weak. The only other time he could remember of his father being this way, was when he had come down with the flu when Kinth was just a teen. Other than this time, he had always been a healthy, lively person.

"What do we do? Doesn't look like he comin' back." Aldo says. "Even his ugly help hasn't been this way."

Kinth glances at the cell gates before saying anything, the stress growing in his brow. Suddenly, a loud roar filled the space, even louder than the roars to which he had grown accustomed to hearing from the beasts that stood guard.

"You thought you could plot against me?! Me!" Sir Grace screams from another part of the prison. His voice traveled throughout every part of the prison. "Kill them all!"

The usual beasts quickly approach the cell accompanied by two even larger creatures. They open the gate and storm inside like a violent wind, moving toward various corners of the space. Randomly grabbing and throwing prisoners, the beasts move about ferociously. Many of the prisoners never saw what was coming, dying instantly.

"Someone ratted on us!" Kinth whispers, squeezing his fists so hard the color of his knuckles changed. "Enrico! Now! Everyone! Attack!"

Jumping to his feet and stretching out his arms widely, Enrico bends his fingers some. He shakes with sweat forming on his brow. Nervousness caused him to struggle with producing results from his ability, but he managed to copy and project an illusion of the inside of the cell. Sadly, the projection is a tad small.

Another prisoner, having similar abilities, notices Enrico's efforts and runs to his aide. Both band together, managing to increase the size of the projection. As a result, they confuse some of the beasts, who think the cell had become empty.

"You three, guard this man!" Kinth said to another small group of prisoners, and points at his father. Kneeling down quickly, Kinth kisses his father on his brow. He rubs his head a couple times, before preparing himself for the attack. "Aldo, here we go! You ready?"

"Always." Aldo leaps forward and away from Kinth, toward the action. Mustering up every bit of strength he had left over from being overpowered by the beast, Aldo trades blows with one of the creatures nearby, who has similar strength and agility like Kinth.

Aldo ducks and spins around the beasts with swift movements, using the other nearby events to his advantage. One of the other prisoners uses his ability to lift one of the beasts, suspending it in the air just before it slams the beast into a wall. Leaping from one of the backs of another beast, Aldo pounds his elbow into the same creature's head, pushing the beast further into the wall. Cracking the stone behind it, the creature's head hangs with a thick fluid oozing from its skull.

"You won't win!" Sir Grace yells.

Two other prisoners, with the ability to generate fire, have managed to create various flames in the cell. Each scares and confuses the beasts on how to maneuver. Using the flames to his advantage, Kinth runs around them at various moments; blindsiding the beasts and catching them off guard with punches.

Without much notice, one of the larger beasts grabs Kinth from behind and slings him across the cell. Kinth's large frame fell against other prisoners, knocking them all against the back wall of the cell. The force of the collision caused several small cracks to appear in the walls, stretching from various corners.

Noticing the cracks, Kinth screams, "Aldo! Enrico!" He pointed to the wall to inform them of what was happening. Then he pointed to the only window in the cell, hoping they would understand his idea without him saying more. "Regroup! Here! Get behind me!"

Jolting around, Aldo notices the cracks forming in the walls and nods. He waves for the remaining prisoners to move back behind Kinth. Enrico pulls one of the injured elderly to the safest area behind the group. Lining up in formation, the prisoners prepare for one last stance against the massive, heinous creatures.

In the back corner, Kinth's father is still being protected by two prisoners. The third has fallen. Struggling, they protected him by bonding their abilities together. Thus, they created a cloak around them. But the cloak had been pierced several times from the battle, causing injury to all of them.

Sighing, Kinth grows tired. A part of him wants to give up, but he has come too far. Moreover, he has committed too much. Lifting his head, he double-checks that every prisoner left standing is behind him. He stood center, with Aldo on his right and Enrico on his left. "Wait for my signal. Then, everyone move against the side walls." he whispers.

Several feet away, one large beast remained with several smaller ones around it. Chewing on the limbs of a fallen prisoner, the beast breathes heavily. Snot blows from its nostrils, and saliva and blood falls from its mouth. The snot falls onto one of the smaller creatures in front of it, as the beast pulls meat from the dead prisoner's bones. The beast lets out one final roar before it leaps forward - stepping on its smaller counterpart, and running toward the prisoners.

The brief standoff is intense. The air feels as if it had thickened around them. The smell of blood, waste and death covered the open space like a blanket. Balling both fists, Kinth crouches, readying himself for the beast's next attack. The other prisoners prepare themselves similarly.

"Hold!" Kinth says.

The beasts get closer.

"I think I'm going to shit myself," a random prisoner moves behind Kinth.

"On me!" Kinth yells again.

The largest of the creatures leaps into the air, just a few feet away in front of Kinth. The other smaller beasts around it continue to run straightforward with much aggression.

"Now!" Kinth hollered, with the veins in his face and neck practically jumping out of his skin.

At this moment, everyone standing behind Kinth split into two groups. All quickly move against the side walls. Kinth, Enrico and Aldo all run toward the beasts, but at calculated moments, they duck and tuck their bodies as they roll into the beasts. This action causes the beast to trip over themselves while they were running.

Slamming into the wall, the largest beast causes the wall to crack more and shatter. It exposes the foggy outdoors around Delrusia Island. With large chunks of concrete falling around it, the beast then shrieks. It realizes that it was no longer safe inside, but instead falling into the darkened depths below the prison.

The remaining creatures were running with so much momentum that, once they were tripped by Kinth and the others, they began to tumble also. Most of them followed the same suit as the larger beast, falling over one another; squealing in fear. For the stragglers, Kinth and the prisoners were able to subdue them with ease. They pushed and tossed out those who remained.

Afterwards, Kinth gleamed with sweat, but he immediately ran to his father's side. He verified that all the creatures were gone before transferring most of his attention to his father. Examining him, he likewise took a look at the two prisoners who had provided the cloak protection over his father. Both of these men were now unconscious, having passed out from using their abilities for such an extended amount of time.

"Father!" Kinth said, grabbing him somewhat aggressively and sliding his head onto his lap. "Father!"

Out of breath, Aldo rushes over with Enrico and others behind him. Aldo notices that more of the prison walls were cracking around them. "Kinth, we need to go – now!"

"Father!" Kinth began to lose his focus as his voice began breaking. He leaned in to listen to his father's breath, which was faint to nothing at all.

"Kinth!" Aldo screams again.

A large piece of the floor cracks some feet away and breaks off. It causes another slab of concrete to fall, taking a few prisoners with it.

"We must go!" Enrico agreed with Aldo's sentiments. He repeated himself in his native tongue again, so that some others like him would understand.

Kinth rises slowly, grabbing and lifting his father almost as if he was a child. He begins to walk to the gate of the cell which had been left ajar.

"What about Sir Grace?" Enrico asked. "There may be more of them."

Aldo said nothing as he bolted in front of Kinth, ensuring he kept an eye out for any future threats. The other prisoners, grateful to be alive and free, followed behind Aldo closely. A wall of battered and bruised people positioned themselves in front of Kinth, thankful for being freed.

"Free the others," Kinth said after some time walking. With a sorrowful tone, he spoke to no one in particular.

Enrico watched in subtle amazement as the prisoners obeyed the order without any issue, almost if Kinth had never left his role as head of The Guardian's security some time ago. The various prisoners separated from the group, visiting the various cells and used their abilities to open the gates. The remaining prisoners, frightened and bewildered, didn't hesitate to run from their confinement. Rather, they blended quickly with the others.

Once outside, the tired group looked around the eerie, dark perimeter. All tried to see as much as they could with the fog around them. Kinth kneeled to the ground just before the gap between the prison platform and the column pathway. He laid his father down and looked over his face, quickly reminiscing on how his father had looked when he was a kid.

A random prisoner ran to his side. Distressed at what he saw, he put both of his hands on his face. "We are so sorry. He was a good man. He protected us and educated us inside, until he became too weak to do so. Were you his son?"

Kinth looked up at the man slowly. With frustration in his eyes, he could only nod.

Shaking his head in sorrow, the prisoner retreats to give Kinth a moment alone.

Without notice, a blaring shriek traveled through the area; loud enough that it shook every structure under its presence. Panicking, the group looked around and above. They noticed the winged beast moving throughout the air.

"Look!" a prisoner shouted, pointing toward the sky.

From the group's vantage point, they could see the silhouette of someone standing at the top of the narrow, jagged steps leading to the prison.

"Did you actually think you were going to leave this place alive? You didn't think that, did you?" Sir Grace shouted from above, clapping his hands slowly.

Chapter 4

EKLADI PEOPLE – BIYO BRIDGE

KIRA STANDS AT THE PATH'S EDGE, WATCHING CLOSELY AS Langston and Jesse continue to progress across the bridge. They move beneath large patches of fungi, vines, and tree branches. The foliage is slightly thicker and greener near the bridge, mostly due to the condensation randomly moving.

Watching them with concerned eyes, Kira unknowingly sways back and forth. She takes a moment to exhale deeply. Her clothing floats and shifts with the passing wind. Gazing at the sky, she notices a sudden darkening that has fallen over the area where she and the other Ekladi people stood.

The sky seemed different to her, but *could it just be exhaustion?* she thinks.

Slowly approaching the rest of her group, Kira looks over her shoulder once more. Then, she notices Langston and Jesse having had completely vanished from her view. The only thing left to see was the entrance opening of the bridge which was between the large, mountainous environment. Continuing her casual pace, Kira is met by some of the other Ekladi people. All are a variety of people of various sizes and abilities.

"Seems another cycle is approaching," a round, balding man wearing a hooded robe says, observing the sky.

"Possibly," Kira responds.

Once back within the group, Kira remains quiet as she picks up her pace. Aggressively she walks in the direction of their home. Deep within in her thoughts, her concentration is broken when another person within her group approaches her, visibly frustrated.

"Kira," the person whispers.

Kira turns her head slightly, her eyebrows raised.

The person gently touches Kira's garment. "What are we doing?"

"What do you mean, Selania? What are we doing about what?" Kira maintains her pace, keeping her focus on the path ahead.

"We have been moving amongst these lands for many cycles, and for what? When will we infiltrate Hock City? Why are we wasting our time and resources to help strangers?" Selania replies.

"Be patient," Kira replies, softly.

"The longer we stay out here, the more people we will lose. This sky looks even more threatening than usual. You aren't the only one -"

Kira jerks around, stepping toward Selania aggressively, while positioning herself just inches away from her face. The others in the group continue to walk ahead. "Be . . . *patient*. I know what you are about to say. You don't have to keep reminding me of our mission. I have not forgotten. We will talk more in our meeting area back home."

Frowning, Selania says nothing. Instead, she storms off, bumping against Kira as she walks away. The others in the group did their best to not pry into the conversation. Still, they couldn't help but watch the brief standoff as they continued to walk ahead.

Back at the Ekladi dwelling, Kira and those who traveled with her are rejoined by other locals. Most of the people are older but there are some young amongst them. The large group gathers in the meeting hall. Kira and a few others sit around the same table they used to explain their history to Langston and Jesse, just before leading them to the bridge.

There is an awkward silence present, mostly because Kira is still profoundly within her thoughts. The others nearby watch her closely, waiting for her or for someone else to speak. Separate conversations begin to stir, growing to an octave in which the Ekladi people normally didn't tolerate.

"Okay! Settle down, everyone! Settle down! Please," one of the elders speaks as quietly as he could, but loud enough for the group to hear him.

Growing restless, the group begins to shout out their concerns. They have similar concerns, such as the ones shared by Selania.

"I know you all have questions." Kira snaps out of her thoughtful gaze, speaking assertively while looking at the center of the table. "And I know you want to know what's next for us. Please. Have a seat somewhere and let's discuss."

The elderly members sit around the table first. Then, the others in the room fill the gaps behind them. Those left standing position themselves closer to the table.

Watching the movement in the room, Kira repositions herself in her seat, studying the various facial expressions of those around her. It's only a small portion of her people. This meeting was not all-encompassing. Selania stands at the other end of the table, her arms folded, and her jaw clenched. Noticing Selania's body language, Kira forms her mouth to speak. But then, she abruptly changes what she had planned to say.

"Before I say what needs to be said, some of you are fairly new to our people; new to our movement. I feel as though it is only right to share a few things first." Kira leans forward, sighing as she rests her arms on the table. "Most of us here once lived inside those walls. Some around this table are old enough to remember how things were before that evil, conniving man took over as leader. The new Guardian is a cruel, self-serving man. He took my mother and made her a servant inside that city - inside his home. As he did to some of your relatives. When my father spoke out about this, he was removed from the city. It has been many cycles since I have seen either of them. I know my mother is alive, but I do not know if the same is for my father. Some of you have similar stories, thus the reason why I believe the universe joined us together.

"I vowed that I would free my mother, and help free any others who are being held inside that city against their will. My plan was to collect as many people and resources and work together against The Guardian. It has taken some time and we have lost some of our people," Kira glances at Selania again. "Sometimes, we have been sidetracked. But the mission has not changed. I have *not* . . . lost sight of what our goal is."

"Then what are we doing?" a voice travels from within the group.

"Yeah! Why did we help those two people?! We only allow ourselves to be seen for what we are - when necessary. That is your rule," another from the group contributes to the topic.

Grumbles of the group begin to elevate again, with various side conversations forming. The anxiousness and anxieties begin to pour from the pores of those around like small holes in a floodgate.

Noticing she was losing control of the conversation, Kira quickly stands to her feet. She slams one of her hands on the table. "Enough! Please! Let me continue!" Her swift change in demeanor startles those near her at the table.

As Kira slowly sits down, the sound of heavy, rapid footsteps travels into the hall before the person they belong to can appear. Excitement grows, causing a natural parting of the crowd and allowing the person to enter into the meeting.

"Kira! Kira!" a young, slim woman walks rapidly into the hall, wearing a hood and a cloth wrapped around half her face. Her eyes were painted darkly. Pushing her way through those unaware of her presence, she made her way to the table. "I have news."

"Can this news wait?" Kira replies.

"No. Well . . . I don't think it should."

Looking around quickly, Kira contemplates whether she wants the entire group to hear the news or not. Asking them to leave the hall with their questions unanswered was a sure way to cause further friction. Concerned by what this news could be; the group around the table quickly directs their attention to the young woman.

"For those who don't know, this is one of our collectors. She travels throughout the Pines for me."

"What is her name?" someone asks.

Before another question could travel across the room, Kira replies, "The names of those who collect for us are private for their protection."

"But we always travel as a group," an elder interrupts, leaning on the table aggressively to show the urgency behind his words. "Why is she traveling alone?"

"She doesn't travel as an Ekladi member. She travels as a local – or as anything she needs to be. I have asked her and some others to find resources and people that could benefit our cause. For her safety, I did not consult with any of you prior. I did not want too many to know . . . again, for their protection," Kira answers confidently.

Displeased grumbles travel across the room.

The collector continues. "Kira, the city is in unrest. Many from inside the walls are now amongst the other people in the Pines. The Guardian seems to be in search of someone."

Those who traveled with Kira to the bridge quickly glanced at each other.

"Anything more?" Kira asks.

"From what I could gather, there are multiple groups looking for the same person for whom The Guardian is looking. So much so, that violence occurred at the local market. I was also able to follow a woman –"

"A woman?" Kira says sharply, leaning on the table.

"Yes. I was traveling south through the flatlands when I noticed her. I found her means of travel . . . odd. So, I followed her and her protectors. She visited a home north of the city. I also saw some others – who appeared to be following her also. Something seemed off about these people. So I didn't hang around too long to see what happened between them at this house."

"You see! This is because of those two you helped!" a woman interrupts the conversation, standing and pointing at Kira. "They have apparently caused trouble in that city! And that trouble could be headed our way! You have put us at risk by bringing them here!"

The slightly quiet gripes from before have now grown to random outbursts and shouting. Kira stares at the table deeply, as if she was searching for solutions in the grains of the table's wood. Standing, she paces slowly around the room.

"Nothing to say?" Selania steps forward, speaking in a smug tone.

Pausing her steps, Kira looks at Selania. Then, Kira quickly scans the room. "As I said . . . my mission has not changed. OUR . . . mission has not changed. I have not forgotten that, just as I, many of you have family who are still being held in that city against their will. All are working like slaves. For some time, we have been waiting for an opportunity to strike – to free them. And I believe . . . I believe . . . we have found it."

"What are you suggesting?" an elderly Ekladi member asks.

Turning around slowly, Kira says, "We attack. But first, let's visit this house located north."

"Why is that necessary?" Selania asks.

"I will share more, but not now. Please. We have already lost time talking. Selania, you are in charge here while I am gone." Kira walks quickly out of the room.

Chapter 5

LANGSTON, JESSE & WINSTON – BIYO BRIDGE

WATER DROPLETS FALL AROUND THE LARGE, ROCKY environment, tapping on the roof of the tower. Drifting down the small windows of the tower slowly, the droplets create a soothing sound that creates a peaceful atmosphere.

This serene moment is quite different than what Langston, Jesse or Winston have seen in recent days. Sleeping much at all was a surprise. The moisture outdoors and body heat in the midst of small quarters created a pleasant, warm space for their weary souls to catch their second wind.

The three positioned themselves at various places in the small room to sleep. Jesse had been sleeping soundly without much movement, his hat covering his face. Although this is not the same luxury as sleeping in his room at Madam Pearl's place, it would have to do for now.

Because of his age and weakening energy, Winston had repositioned himself several times on the cot during this break in their travels. Snoring loudly, he coughs and grumbles at times while saying incomprehensible words in his sleep. He strokes his long, gray beard. This seems to relax him enough for him to fall back asleep.

Lying parallel to an adjacent wall is Langston, asleep like the others. He is a bit quieter than Winston, but not sleeping as soundly as Jesse. Turning his body randomly, Langston ends up on his side and facing the wall. Frowning while he sleeps, something heavy is on his mind.

An intense silence briefly falls over the room. With the exception of the sounds of falling water, as well as snoring and heavy breathing, not much else could be heard. Langston seemed to fall back into the grasp of whatever had him when he and Jesse first started crossing the bridge. An awful dream that seemed to hold him like a creature, refusing to let go.

Turning his head at first, Langston moans uncontrollably. His body shakes, while he mouths something to himself. It appears that he is fully submerged into his dream. It had begun to stress his mind and body as he slept, causing him to jerk and move on the floor.

In the first part of the dream, he is lying on something – a bed perhaps – but the vision is not clear to him. His arms are bound, and he is also asleep in the dream. When he awakens within the dream, there are silhouettes of people in the shadows, all staring at him. He speaks to the people in the dream aloud while he is still under. "What is this? Who are you?" he says, turning and jerking his body. His eyes move rapidly, as he screams out in the dream. It causes himself to awaken.

Awake now, Langston nervously examines the room. He notices that he was safe and just dreaming. Despite the brief commotion, Jesse and Winston didn't budge. Lying back down, Langston breaths in and out deeply before closing his eyes once more. He slowly reentered a deep sleep.

Then, a new dream begins.

This dream consisted of the time when Langston was a teen, sitting in his room at his home. He is sitting on his bed and reading a comic. Sometimes, he was listening to his mother talk to one of her friends – a woman with a hefty laugh – in the other room. Langston isn't really paying the two much mind, but every now and then, he holds onto a phrase or two.

"Well, it sho is good to have someone new in the building that I can talk to," the woman says.

"Yes, girl. I'm glad we met," Langston's mother replies.

"Now tell me again – how did you come to get to this ole place?"

A loud crash fills the room.

The crash in the dream awakes Langston once more, causing him to gaze at the ceiling. He listens to the sound of droplets tapping against the tower. Struggling to get back to sleep, he turns on his side again. He continues watching Jesse and the old man sleep heavier than him. Sighing, he closes his eyes and tries again, but the dreams continue.

In the next dream, Langston is running down dimly lit hallways. Unsure on where he is going and how to get out, he runs as fast as he can. Sometimes he is slamming into walls because he doesn't know where the exits are. He often looks over his shoulder, mouthing inaudible words. At times, he yells, 'No!' to whoever is running behind him. These screams suddenly become audible, even while he is asleep.

"Mr. Langston," Jesse says, kneeling over Langston. "Mr. Langston! Mr. Langston!" Jesse continues, shaking him a little.

Startled awake, Langston slides away from Jesse.

"It's okay. You were dreaming again," Jesse adds.

Patting Jesse on the leg and nodding, Langston lies down again. He hopes to fall asleep once more but without the dreams. Jesse goes back to his corner of the room and lies down himself.

Sometime later, Langston wakes up to an empty room. Slowly rising to one leg, he kneels and rubs the sleep from the corner of his eyes. The room is much cooler than before, with the moisture drying some around the tower. The warmth has escaped as well.

Looking out of the tower windows, Langston notices Winston casually leaning on one of the guard ropes that were connected between the columns of the bridge.

"Mr. Langston! Wake up! Let's go!" Jesse shouts, walking up the tower stairs rapidly and thinking that Langston was still asleep.

"I'm up, I'm up," Langston responds, groggily.

Jesse stands at the doorway, watching Langston gather his bearings. "We're ready to go," he says.

"Yes, young Langston! Let us move while the time is right!" Winston shouts from below, while listening to the other two. His voice travels across the bridge, bouncing off the large stones around it.

Standing to his feet, Langston stretches his arms tall and exhales deeply. He does his best to release some tension caused by his dreams. He couldn't tell if he actually got any rest after dealing with his dreams that interrupted his sleep most of the night.

Langston notices Jesse, who seemed to be standing still in the doorway and staring at him. He raises his eyebrows, wondering if Jesse had something to say.

"What?" Jesse asks.

"Why are you looking at me like that?"

Jesse shrugs.

"Did I do something in my sleep?" Langston asks, pausing his movements.

Jesse nods.

Langston walks toward him, patting him on the shoulder as he slid by him through the doorway. "Let's go," he said without further talking about the subject.

Jesse studies the floor as if he had more to say.

Gradually walking down the tower's staircase, Langston looks in both directions of the bridge. He sees nothing more than the same shadows from before. Small amounts of light pierce through the large stone structure. A cool wind lightly caresses his face.

"If we go now, we should make it to the end of this rickety bridge before tiring again," Winston says.

Jogging a bit to catch up, Langston replies, "Are you sure you know which way to go?"

Winston continues his pace without responding. Jesse had been listening to the short exchange from the stairs, scribbling a doodle on one of the dusty windows. Quickly he leaps down multiple stairs at a time, rejoining the others. He runs up to walk alongside the old man.

"Is that a yes?" Langston adds, after his first question was met with silence.

"Come! Come! Have faith!" Winston replies, waving a hand.

Traveling the course, the three adjusted to the various inclines and dips from the deteriorating bridge. Several gaps, which were created by mangled and broken wood, made the bridge seem as if it would give way. Regardless, the three maintained a steady pace forward.

A moment of quiet had fallen between them before Langston's thoughts began to run wild. Some of the thoughts were questions. To break the awkward silence, he shared one of his questions. "What was that place like? Like, before the way it is now?"

"What place? Hock?"

"Yeah. You know . . . before –"

"Before the violence and the madness? And the *greed*?" Winston interrupts, stretching out his words somewhat sarcastically.

Alerted by the question, Jesse moves in a bit closer. He had drifted some, in awe by his surroundings.

"Yeah. Like – like . . . can you tell me how it was?" Langston adds.

"My mind grows old with each step I take it seems. Though I can tell you as much as my energy will allow." The old man takes a deep breath, moving his eyes around a bit as if his thoughts were fighting on which words would be spoken next. "Well . . . let's see. I'm not sure what to tell you. Therefore, I will tell you what comes to me."

Continuing to walk, Langston turns his head toward Winston attentively. Jesse has drifted again but was not far behind. He was touching the long vines and various fungi along the ropes of the bridge.

"I haven't always been the man that you see in front of you. I was once young . . . and energetic! And normal. Back when Pineville was one large city, it was divided into smaller regions."

"Regions?" Langston asks.

"Yes. The regions were just large neighborhoods of different people. Many, many people. There were wealthy people in various areas, and others who were less fortunate. Many of these neighborhoods had names, but after the events which have changed us, so changed the names. Now, most of these areas don't have any names. But a few of them were claimed by people and given *new* names." Winston says, smiling reminiscently.

"Like Hock City?"

"No, no. Hock City didn't exist back then. This city was built after the events. The original Guardian wanted to restore the Pines back to normal as much as he could. Because of his leadership, the people began building the city without him even having to ask. They saw his efforts and –"

"They believed in him," Langston interrupts.

"Yes! They did! It took many cycles to build that city. They had to gather as many resources as they could find, tools especially, but more importantly, people. People who knew how to do specific things. Handy people. At first, it took some time to build many of the structures. But once people realized their new abilities, they used them to build things faster. Like the walls that you have seen. Those walls around the city, in fact, were built to lock in the rain that fell in the beginning. But eventually, they found a new use for them. There were many threats growing outside of the walls. So, they made them taller."

"The Ekladi people? The Desert Dwellers?"

"No, no. I have always known of their true identity. That name is a horrible one." Winston strokes his beard softly. "There are other threats in our midst. There are other lands to which I wouldn't dare travel. Lands that probably have the same evils – the same people - that once held you captive before you were able to free yourself."

Nothing more is said by the two for a few moments.

Reigniting the conversation without warning, Winston says, "While the Guardian wanted to restore peace and rebuild where we lived, there were others who went other ways and did the opposite. They built things to prolong the changes created by the event."

"What was it like before all this?" Jesse finally pays attention long enough to form a question for his elder.

Chuckling, Winston pats Jesse on the head. "The Guardian and I were neighbors before the event. We were much younger men. We lived in a quiet, modest neighborhood. As you have noticed, my house still stands."

"That has always been your home?!" Jesse asks excitedly.

"Yes. Yes. Throughout all of the chaos, I managed to keep it standing. Using my abilities, of course. And up until recently, I had . . . peace," Winston cocks an eye at Langston, smiling. "Anyway. On some weekends, The Guardian - before he held such a title - he would help me build or repair things at my home. He was always good with his hands. My wife trusted his skills more than mine sometimes. I was more into business and planning. When the event happened, I was actually at my office. Everything went black outside while I was working. We all ran outside and looked around."

"What was outside? Did you see anything?" Langston asks.

"No one really knows. Because whatever it was . . . was surrounded by fog. Some sort of mist that kept it hidden. And no one wanted to get close to it. Eventually it started to gradually decay and disappeared. But it did a lot of damage, ripping our lands apart and changing people."

Jesse, who had been walking ahead at the moment, stopped suddenly to say something aloud. But because he was a ways ahead, Langston and the old man couldn't hear what he said.

"Hey! What do you see?" Langston interrupts Winston's story, shouting at Jesse.

"Not sure." Jesse points ahead as the other two slowly approach where he is standing. All three of them notice a rickety sign, standing tall but mangled in some places. The arrow portions of the signs were twisted and not mounted as they once were. As such, the three were confused on which way to go. Making matters worse, the wording on the arrows had been scraped off.

"So . . . which way?" Langston says, sighing.

Chapter 6

THE GUARDIAN & TEAM - FLATLANDS

THE LAND WAS ASCENDING IN THIS PARTICULAR PART OF the Pines, becoming bleaker and more challenging to travel. But the Guardian and his unit stay their course. The group traverses a wide desolate area of deserted businesses and bungalows, in what seemed to be an unclaimed strip of land.

Perplexed by the emptiness of the area, The Guardian wonders why he was just noticing what seemed to be an expansive and available area of land upon which he could build. While he examines the vicinity, the news from Mathias moves throughout his mind, disturbing him greatly. At this point, he hopes to stumble upon anyone with information about anything. He is unconcerned about the growing anguish of his men. Their travels are beginning to visibly tire them.

Feeling the pains himself, The Guardian's thoughts are more of a discomfort than the aches of his body. *Is Mathias up to something? Did the Mantis betray The Guardian's orders about the trades with Mathias? Did The Guardian forget to tie up some loose ends?* Wondering about all of this, as well as the whereabouts of his uncle and the human, The Guardian clenches his jaw. He aggressively moves about the flatland path, aggravated by all of the patches of stone and brush in his way.

"Sir! Sir!" One of The Guardian's men shouts out to him. "Can we rest here for a while?" Without waiting for a response, he sits down. He drops his backpack to the ground. After letting out a sigh of relief, he looks up over his shoulder at The Guardian, who surprisingly has his weapon drawn and pointed in his direction.

"Did I say that you could rest? That anyone could rest?" The Guardian looks around and waves his weapon erratically, with a glare from the sky in his eyes. He forms his mouth to say something more but stops abruptly to look up. There he notices the odd change in color and depth of darkness. He walks around the area speechlessly, mouthing something to himself.

"Now that's odd," one of his men says, looking up also.

"Let's move. We will break at a better location," The Guardian storms away, still glancing up sporadically.

Cursing under his breath, the guard who had been sitting stands and gathers his things.

"Sir, I have picked up a scent. Looks like . . . looks like it is going this way," another from the unit interrupts.

Changing their course some, The Guardian follows the guidance of his tracker. He continues to walk through the small city, climbing the rough mountainous land upon which the buildings had been built. For the moment, the city seemed like a ghost town. Only the sounds of the wind blowing against loosely hanging windows and doors could be heard.

Sounds of aggressive footsteps grow nearer. Stopping, The Guardian's men draw their weapons. They formed a partial circle around their leader. Without warning, The Guardian and his unit are surrounded by a small group of odd-looking, smelly locals. People who had even the weirdest people from Hock City beat if there were an ugly contest.

"Looks like we got visitors, Ma," a man says to a woman walking slowly nearby.

"Well, now. I think you might be right about that." A petite, old woman responds with a voice that didn't quite match her appearance. Walking toward The Guardian, she continues, "Give me everything you have. Including whatever is in your pockets and those bags. And don't make me say it again." Wearing an aging leather vest, with tattoos covering her arms and part of her face, the woman rubs her completely shaven head. She doesn't appear to have any weapons on her, with the exception of a large knife hanging from her hip.

Standing at various points in the small city are members of her group. All are armed with metal pipes, baseball bats and more makeshift weapons; dressed similarly to their apparent leader. Some within this group position themselves on top of buildings and cars, or inside doorways and windows. The others have chosen to stay nearby, ready to assist their leader if necessary.

The Guardian turns around slowly to the sound of the woman's voice. He looks at the peculiar, old woman with his eyebrows raised. Then, he looks at the others standing by her. Smiling a smug smile, he lets out an unruly laugh that continues for an oddly long time. He moves around erratically, giving the appearance that he isn't of sound mind.

Frowning, the old woman moves a couple steps closer. "Are you hard of hearin' or somethin'? Did you lose your common sense somewhere in these fields on yo' way here?"

Abruptly ending his laughter, The Guardian bolts toward the woman. He attempts to startle her, but to no avail. Not getting the reaction he wanted, he looks her over – including glancing over her shoulder to get a look at her people – before speaking. "Do you know who I am?"

Spitting at the ground before responding, the woman scoffs, "I don't really care who you are."

The Guardian chuckles at the woman's response. "You hear that, guys? She don't care . . . *who* I am." His unit joins in, snickering at The Guardian's display of confidence. "Tell you what," The Guardian attempts to reach for the woman's shoulder. But before he can touch her, she quickly grabs him by his wrist and slings him across the ground. The act causes him to slide a few feet away. Dirt and debris flies through the air.

Coughing, The Guardian is in shock while his team quickly comes to his aid. They point their weapons at the old woman and those near her, causing a tense standoff. But the actions of The Guardian's men neither seemed to faze the woman nor her people.

Not to mention the size of her group. From first glance, the numbers seemed a bit unequal to the naked eye. The

Guardian had more support with him, and so it initially didn't seem like a fair fight. But there was no telling what was hiding behind the drabby-looking people they faced, especially where they were.

Without warning, the old woman took another step forward. She slammed the bottom of her fist onto the ground, causing the soil and stone to quake and crack under her hand. The crack stretched close to where The Guardian was sitting, pulling the ground apart. Smirking, the woman snickered while looking up. Once again, she raised her hands in threatening fashion. Looking at The Guardian, she cocked one of her eyebrows. Flustered, The Guardian seemed to be frozen in his position.

"Empty your shit," the old woman says fiercely. "Or I will send you down to the core of this land."

More of her people flank The Guardian. One man wore nothing more than boxer briefs with holes in it. He had tall knee-high boots and a backpack – wielding a long, spiked pole. Another woman with purple hair, and part of her face painted, circled around The Guardian. She brandished a metallic, jagged bow with arrows.

The Guardian stood to his feet, dusting himself off. Smiling again, he snapped his fingers and nodded at his unit. His men began to fire their weapons at the old woman and her group. Some of them used their abilities, attacking the new enemies from a distance.

The odd, old woman, upon growing irritated, is surprised at The Guardian's response to attack. Shouting something to her people, the woman slams her fist again and causes an even louder explosion of the ground. This time, the blow is so hard and loud that the sound and vibration traveled over the hills. It causes stones to break apart and roll down several hills into the area where they stood.

At the same moment, the Ekladi people travelled near one of the hills, and had journeyed from the opposite direction. Kira was in hot pursuit after having abruptly ended the council meeting because of the news of activity in the north.

Rumbling from the nearby standoff brought the Ekladi people to alert. "Kira, did you feel that?" one of them asked. More inaudible questions and mumbles from the group occurs.

Turning toward the direction of the sounds, Kira quickly jogs up one of the hills without warning. Crouching as she climbs it, she motions instructions to her group. Those traveling with her who possessed specific abilities positioned themselves at opposite ends of the hill, providing a camouflaged cloak around everyone.

Lying on the ground at the peak of the hill, Kira looks down at the activity below. From her vantage point, she could see two groups of people that appeared to be at the beginning stages of a fight. Motioning her hand at another member within her group, she instructs a young woman to use her abilities. The woman closes her eyes for a moment. Then, she seemed to have disappeared while returning moments later.

"What could you see?" Kira whispers to the woman.

Slightly out of breath, the woman replies, "I could only get so close. I started to get winded climbing the stones below. But The Guardian —"

"The Guardian?!" another Ekladi woman interrupts hastily.

"Shh. Shh," Kira slides closer to the young woman.

"Yes. The Guardian is down there."

Gently grabbing the woman by both arms, Kira asks, "Are you sure?"

"Yes. I wasn't able to verify much more. I didn't want to risk reappearing too soon, or getting us caught."

"That was wise of you," Kira replies, emphatically. "Could you hear any of the words being exchanged? What were they talking about?"

"Nothing important from what I could tell."

Kira ponders for a moment.

"So . . . now what?" an Ekladi lieutenant approaches the others.

Looking down the hill at the activity, Kira squints her eyes to see as much as she could. The Guardian and his unit were scattered about. They were fighting the other group of people from various places within the small city. All the commotion caused a film of dirt to fill the air, making it hard for anyone to see clearly.

"If The Guardian is down there, that means the city is possibly unmanned and vulnerable," the lieutenant adds passionately.

The group studies the activity more.

"Create a distraction, everyone. It will hopefully deter that other group," Kira says before turning her attention to the lieutenant. "You and I, we will greet The Guardian thereafter. Hopefully we can keep him out here long enough. We need him distracted."

"Distracted?" another Ekladi person asks, probingly.

"Yes. Head back. Advise the others on what we have seen here. Tell them that I said to send a group to the flatlands. Be ready for a battle. We will meet you there. Don't do anything until we reconnect."

Nodding, the Ekladi member runs off with several others following behind her.

"Everyone, quickly. Create a Tanglier that will scare off those people!" Kira whispers energetically.

Two other members come close to one another, standing side by side. Joining hands, the two of them cocked their heads up toward the sky and closed their eyes tightly. Inhaling deeply, they pull a blanket of the air and sand into their bodies. They moved it around within them forcefully, creating a large, desert creature. The same type of creature that Langston originally saw when he first met the Ekladi people off Highway 99, but even larger in size this time.

The two Ekladi people became concealed within the sand monster but could still communicate to those around them. They could also control the object's movement, as if it was a large puppet.

"Go to the top of the hill. We will go around and flank them. Everyone else, use your abilities to support the others. Move the soil and the stones," Kira orders.

As the two control the large sand creature, moving it slowly up the hill, Kira and the others move to a new vantage point. They move in segments, hiding behind large stones until they got close enough to the action between The Guardian and the unknown group of people.

Pausing for a moment, Kira and the others watch The Guardian's men go head-to-head with the new apparent enemy. The old woman has managed to frustrate The Guardian with her abilities, and her counterparts were just as annoying. They make loud, strange noises as they oddly move about, but they otherwise seemed skillfully trained.

Reaching the top of the hill, The Tanglier positions itself just above where the battle is happening. It casts an even larger shadow onto the area already darkened by the sky, with a little lighting piercing through the eyes of it.

"Desert Dwellers!" one of the people with the old woman screams, pointing toward the hill.

Without warning, the old woman runs away. Her people follow closely behind her. Everyone else in the vicinity turns their attention to the large sand creature slowly making its way down the hill. The wind stirs near the creature, moving the sand around it wildly and rapidly.

Panicking, The Guardian's unit immediately begins to fire at the Tanglier. Even though they shoot their weapons wildly, they don't manage to hit anything. The sand consumes everything they fire its way.

Jumping onto a large stone, The Guardian screams, "Retreat! But stay together and continue our course!"

Moving hastily toward the original path, The Guardian's unit make a quick getaway. But The Guardian has other plans. Pretending to run behind his team, he ducks into one of the old rooms inside of a building. Then, he lowers himself down below a windowpane. He watches as his men make it over one of the adjacent hills before coming back out.

"Okay! Okay! Kira! I know you are out here somewhere!" he shouts, with both of his hands near his mouth.

"What are you doing out here?!" Kira responds loudly, as she came from behind a large patch of brush. "That will be all," she says to those with her, who had been controlling the Tanglier.

With a swift motion, the sand falls to the ground and dismantles the sand monster.

The Guardian approaches Kira slowly, ensuring with his eyes that it was safe. "What information do you have for me?"

"How is my mother?" Kira replies, sternly. "When will you release her and the others?"

At first, The Guardian does not respond. He tilts his head in an arrogant fashion, squinting his eyes at Kira. He glances at her people before pacing in front of her. "Your mother is safe," he finally replies.

"If you harm her –"

"You are in no position to threaten me," The Guardian interjects, dusting off his clothing.

"But we just saved you from a sure loss!"

"Silence!"

Bowing her head, Kira searches for patience and control over her words.

"Remember, you must give me anything I ask. Only then will your mother and the others stay safe inside my walls," The Guardian continues.

"It has been many cycles. And my people have served you as you have required. Please. Release her to me. Let me trade places with her." Kira softens her tone in her reply.

"Your mother's abilities are far more useful than you."

Shaking her head, Kira pleads more. "But she is one of many. There are others with her abilities. Plenty amongst these lands."

The Guardian paces around the area leisurely. "What information do you have for me?"

Kira sighs heavily, "The usual stragglers. But one of my people saw an old man."

"An old man?" The Guardian says, stopping in his tracks.

"Yes."

"And where did this *old man* . . . go?"

"He headed over those hills," Kira points. "We are unsure where he was going."

In reference, the hills were around the same path in which The Guardian was already planning to travel. Smiling, The Guardian starts to walk away. "I will let your mother know that you are well."

Fuming, Kira watches as The Guardian leaves the area. She stares at him scornfully. Her pain coursed through her veins so deeply that she shed a tear. Exhaling, she immediately walked north toward the flatlands in the direction of Hock City.

"Won't we bring harm to the human by sending The Guardian in that direction?" one of her people asks, worriedly.

Looking away shamefully, Kira replies, "My concern is only of my mother and the others from our families inside of that wall. Maybe Selania is right. Maybe I have been distracted. Besides, I believe that the human will be okay."

"How are you so certain?"

Taking a moment to respond, Kira observes the area in front of her. "Just a feeling. We must worry about one thing at a time," she says.

Chapter 7

SADIE BELL LOUNGE – HOCK CITY

THE SADIE BELL LOUNGE HOSTED A DIFFERENT CROWD FOR the moment. Before the chaos caused by the rare human sighting, various people of Hock City would frequent Sadie Bell's to hear live music and consume ale – amongst other substances. Mostly the older, adult crowd. But sometimes, young ones would sneak in through the loose venting on the rooftop and work their way down a hatch that led to a walkway used for those who managed the lighting. This allowed them to watch the action on the main level from above. Until they were caught, of course.

Nobody got anything for free in the city. *Everything* had its cost.

Currently, the music is silent in the venue and the crowd is gone. They have been moved out amongst everyone else – on the opposite side of the walls. With the exception of a few of the staff that hid and managed to not be discovered during the evacuation, the original faces were no longer around. Now it was just a handful of people, bound at the wrists and ankles. Everyone sat in front of two faces they hadn't seen before: Sam and Rahzy.

The two bounty hunters managed to sneak inside the city with the help from Madam Pearl. Assistance she didn't want to provide - but as their captive - she hadn't any choice. She showed them a secret entrance that she normally ordered Jesse to use whenever possible. Therefore, he could discreetly get in and out of the city due to his runs throughout the Pines. Routes Jesse rarely used because the tunnels became his favorite after Miles showed them to him.

Inside of Sadie Bell's was a large, open area with various seating around an elevated, circular stage. Dark red painted walls, pink couches and the aroma of lust, greed as well as Kush incense covered the room. Figurines and paintings were positioned neatly on the walls.

Madam Pearl is bound to a chair on the stage with her head hanging, within a deep slumber. Various workers who had been discovered hiding inside of the lounge are bound individually to other chairs. Each are physically spaced out across one wall of the venue.

Sam paces behind a long bar adjacent to the stage, helping himself to various flavors of ale and peanuts left out before the commotion. He gazes at the paintings on the wall. Abstract bodies, devices and shapes. Stopping, he looks into a mirror and notices Rahzy staring at him.

"You know . . . we aren't going to get anything done in this city if you keep drinking like that," Rahzy says, lounging back in his chair enough that it tilts on its back legs. "And how long are we going to let this ole broad sleep?"

Smacking his lips from the potent taste of the ale, Sam glances at Rahzy before tossing more peanuts into his mouth. Though, Sam doesn't reply immediately. Instead, he walks over to one of the workers who is practically asleep himself, slapping him one hard time across the face.

"Hey! Wake up!" Sam shouts as quietly as he could. He kneels in front of him. "And if you scream . . . *if you scream*, I will kill ya. Make it easy on yourself. Mm'kay?"

The man – a hybrid of human and fox, but with only slight physical attributes of fox – slowly comes to himself. Shaking his head, he brings attention to his ears which are larger than normal. His facial hair is thick, evidently fur that had been trimmed to appear as a beard. "What do you want with us?"

"Nothin.' But if you want to get outta here at some point, you will answer my questions." Sam begins to pace again. "What is this place?"

"Sadie Bell's."

Frowning, Sam scratches his chin. "Sadie what?"

"You don't know about Sadie Bell's?" The man lifts his head in surprise, looking over at his co-workers. "This place is where people come to unwind. You already tasted the drinks. They normally have music and a little fun in the backrooms."

"*Fun*," Sammy scoffs.

"Does the man in charge ever come here?" Rahzy chimes in, bringing his chair down to the floor.

"The man? In charge? Sadie Bell runs this place, and she definitely ain't no man. But she is never here."

"No, fool. The man that runs this city. What did she call him, Rah?" Sam says, turning his head.

"The Gatekeeper. No. Gov – no! Guardian!"

"Yeah. That's right."

"The Guardian? Man, no. Never seen that man in person. Only on them flyers all through the street. He doesn't come in here. Why would a man like that come to this hole-in-the-wall?"

Shrugging, Sammy returns to pacing around the venue. He peeks out one of the tinted windows on the main wall by the entrance. There, he notices Hock City guards casually walking the nearby perimeters.

Rahzy hops to his feet, joining Sammy by the window. "How long are we goin' to wait here? This guy may never come back. And the amount of security out there seems to be growing."

"How long y'all gonna keep us tied up? I need to pee!" Madam Pearl startles the workers near her, surprising Sammy and Rahzy with her loud, boisterous request which came out of nowhere.

"Well, well. Look who it is, Rah. The Queen of this odd city!"

"I thought she said she was his sister, right? So she can't be the queen. Wouldn't that make her —"

Stroking his forehead, Sam interjects, "Shut up, Rah!"

"I said I need to pee!" Madam Pearl moves aggressively in her chair, rocking it and causing it to scrape the floor.

"How do we get your brother back here? Tell me and I will let you go pee," Sam says, after pulling up a chair. He sits in front of Madam Pearl on the floor, just before the stage.

"I will pee right here! Test me if you want. I ain't playin'."

Laughing, Sam says, "Go 'head! It will be you sittin' in your own piss, not me. And these fine employees of this dump will have to clean up your mess."

The staff look at each other disgustingly.

Madam Pearl sighs before trying to free herself, grunting as she attempts to pull her hands free. "What do you want? Please! I gotta pee!"

"Your brother knows where the human is. So . . . how do we get him back here? So we can . . ." Sammy looks over at Rahzy smugly, ". . . talk. All we want is information on how to find the human."

Mouthing the word 'human' quietly, the staff look at each other again, shockingly.

"Hmph," Madam Pearl looks up at the ceiling and back at Sam. She stares at him with an unbothered facial expression. "You ain't get nothin' more outta me until I use the ladies room."

"Man, take this broad to the bathroom," Sam sighs, pointing at one of the staff whom was still tied up. "You! You take her."

Rahzy walks over and with a quick motion, severing the cloth that was used to bind the young woman employee to the chair. The woman is so nervous, however, that her breathing is heavy. It's to the point that Rahzy takes notice of her large, sweaty bosom moving up and down.

"Rah!"

"Oh! Sorry!" Rahzy replies, before walking over to Madam Pearl and releasing her.

"Go with 'em, Rah. You already know what to do if she tries to run."

An awkward silence falls throughout the room. Pearl moves her large frame down the stage and follows behind the young woman. Stopping for a moment, Pearl has more to say but needs to gather her thoughts. "If you want my brother," she says, turning around, "Mantis knows where he is."

"Who the hell is that?" Sam replies.

Madam Pearl shuffles faster toward the bathroom, stopping again. Wiggling a little to control her bladder, she says, "When y'all looked out those windows, did you see security outside? If you did, then Mantis isn't far away. Now move, chump!" She pushes Rahzy to the side.

Shaking his head, Sam let out a light chuckle as he watched Pearl walk away. Then, he walked back toward the front of the venue. He leaned over the bar to grab a bottle of ale for another sip. "You . . . if I let you go – you gotta do one thing for me."

Another employee nods his head rapidly, practically shivering enough to make his chair move across the room.

"Use your words. Say: 'Okay, I will.'"

"I will, yes – please. Okay. Got it," the young man with a thin mustache and glasses replies. The lines in his face flicker because of his nervousness.

Sighing, Sam says, "When I let you go, I need you to run to one of those guards outside. Tell them that some strange people are inside this Sadie Bell place. Tell them that they have The Guardian's sister hostage. Then, tell them the people want to see Mateo."

"Mantis!" another employee chimes in.

"Whatever! Mantis! Sheesh, this fuckin' place," Sam rubs his brow. "Got it?"

The young man nods again.

Coming around the bar, Sammy approaches the man and removes the cloth binding him. Standing, the young man dusts off his shirt and looks at Sammy nervously.

"Give me your arm," Sam orders, holding out his hand.

Apprehensively, the young man doesn't move.

"Your arm, dude," Sam says again, watching as the young employee raises his slightly. He holds his trembling arm out in front of him. Reaching into his pocket, Sam pulls out a round, mechanical device. He loosens the latch of it and holds it over the man's arm. The device attaches itself to the man's arm, delivering a couple small beeping sounds thereafter. "Now. This . . . this is a tracking device. If you don't do what I ask, I will use it to find you at some point. You can't remove it. If you try, it will do some things. And you will die. But if you DO . . . what I ask, I will deactivate it. Then, it will fall right off your arm. Free and clear. Understand?"

Nodding again, the young man bolts out the double doors of the venue. He runs a couple blocks away down the street.

Watching the man through the window, Sam smirks as he hears the footsteps of Rahzy and Madam Pearl making their way back toward the stage. Sam shouts to Rahzy without turning his attention away from outside. "I see she didn't fall in. That would have been one hell of a mess."

"Fuck you, jerk," Pearl wipes her hands with a towel.

Chuckling, Rahzy says, "That would have been a sight to see."

"Make sure you tie her back up tightly. And put those other ones around her."

"What's the plan?" Rahzy asks.

Turning around slowly, Sam replies, "We should have visitors shortly."

Several moments later, a thunderous sound rattles the front part of the venue. Paintings, figurines, and miscellaneous debris shake, causing some to fall to the floor.

Sam looks outside again. What appeared to be a small army of guards were strategically lining up and down the street in front of the venue. Some were positioned inside four-wheeled machines that were equipped with heavy artillery. Sam also sees another small group of guards conversing, but can't make out what they are saying.

Outside, the unit shouted orders to one another. "Position yourself around the perimeter. Ensure that we have eyes on all the exits." The captain says. "No one do anything until The Mantis arrives."

Another smaller guard with only three long fingers on each hand steps forward, holding a bullhorn. "Not sure who is in there, or how you manage to get in here. I honestly don't care. But come out and you won't get hurt. We will just throw you outside the walls like everyone else." The guard says with a slithery voice.

Inside Sadie Bell's, Sammy sneers at the guard's comments, but doesn't respond.

Joining him, Rahzy looks at what was brewing outside of the venue. "There's too many of them," he says. "Much more than out in those fields."

"Relax. We aren't goin' to fight," Sam replies.

"He damn right he ain't gon' fight, cause Mantis don't play! He will destroy y'all!" Madam Pearl interjects.

"Keep talkin,' thickums – and I will gag you."

Outside, the thunderous force of guards moving into a different formation shook the ground. The Mantis walks down an aisle between the army, making his way to where the captain was standing in front of Sadie Bell's. Leaning in toward the ear of the captain, the two exchanged inaudible words as Sammy and Rahzy maintained a close eye on what was happening from inside of the venue.

Rahzy starts to check his weapons, loading up a couple of sidearms. Meanwhile, he activates and deactivates his energy shield. The sound of it surprises Sam, causing him to make a frustrated expression toward Rahzy.

"What? Gotta always stay ready," Rahzy says.

Walking toward the venue's entrance, The Mantis is stopped by the guard with the bullhorn. The guard extends the bullhorn toward The Mantis, but his offer is declined. "I won't be needing that," The Mantis says confidently. Approaching the doors of the venue, he straightens his clothing and clears his throat.

Inside, Sam taps Rahzy on the shoulder, pointing through the window.

"Whoever you are, let's talk. I can assure you we can both end this rather quickly without anyone getting hurt," The Mantis says with assertion.

Rahzy takes a few steps back and draws his weapon, alarming Sam.

"No, no, no. Go over there. Stand in front of them. We are just talking . . . for now, " Sam aggressively whispers.

As Rahzy walks away, Sam unlocks the door - backing away from it as it slowly drifts open. The Mantis takes a few steps inside, examining the room some before standing still in the lobby area. "I need to know that Pearl is okay," he eventually says.

"Or . . . what?" Sam replies.

The Mantis raises one of his hands, extending one of his fingers. Behind him, one of the guards loads a large weapon with rectangular cartridges. After loading, the weapon opens and several barrels extend, pointing directly at the venue.

"I have no problem leveling this place with you in it."

"No need for that, Mantis. I'm alright. Just tired of being tied up and almost having to pee on myself!" Madam Pearl interjects.

"Seeeee! She's fine. For now. You can kill us, yes. But we will end her before that can happen," Sammy says. He raises one of his devices in the air – the same type of device he put on the young employee moments ago. One was also on Madam Pearl's wrist.

Growing frustrated, Mantis asks, "Who are you?"

Sammy crosses his arms. "Our names are not important."

"Then who do you work for?"

"We work for ourselves."

Nodding his head slowly, The Mantis crosses his arms. "Ahh. Bounty hunters."

"How'd you guess that?"

"The way you're dressed. Your tools. Your weapons. It wasn't hard to piece together."

Repositioning himself, Rahzy says, "We were looking for someone else in this city when we found out about your human problem."

The Mantis turns his head, doing his best to not act stunned at the fact that the bounty hunters knew about the human too.

"Yeah, we know."

"And? What do you want?" Mantis asks.

Smiling, Sam replies, "What do you think?"

"The human?"

"Yeah. Or information on his whereabouts. We can make a pretty good bounty off 'em. Your friend back there confessed that her brother knows where he is. So, the human or your boss. One or the other."

"Well, there is no human here. So, speaking with The Guardian, you say that this will suffice?"

Sammy shrugs. "It will *suffice*, should he have some real information on his whereabouts."

Pacing slowly, The Mantis glances out the window. Then, he moves toward where Pearl and the others were sitting. Eventually he pauses his stroll, choosing to stand directly in front of Sammy.

"Let me save you some time and energy. The Guardian doesn't know where the human is. That is the reason why this city is in disarray. He is not here and will not return for many cycles."

"Where is he then?" Rahzy asks.

"He didn't tell me where he was going, but I assure you that he wants no part of this human." The Mantis takes a long pause. "What if I made you an offer? One that would be just as satisfying as finding the human?"

"Don't waste my time," Sammy snaps back, irritatingly.

"I assure you that this is not a game."

"Better listen to him! The Mantis keeps his word!" Madam Pearl shouts.

Sammy looks over his shoulder, giving a signal for silence to Rahzy. Rahzy then leaps onto the stage and unsheathes one of his short swords, placing it on Pearl's chest.

Clicking a button on the device, Sammy turns his attention back to The Mantis, "Is that true? You keep your word?"

"Our word is our bond. Yes?" Mantis says, looking over Sammy's shoulders and raising one of his hands. He notices the sword. "No need for any of that, sir. I promise you that my offer will be worth your while. Please remove the blade from the madam."

Watching Sam's body language closely, Rahzy also studies the Mantis' behavior. He scans him as if he is looking for a lie hidden somewhere within his clothing. Growing tired of talking, he jumps off the stage and approaches the Mantis aggressively.

"Rah, stand down. Give us a moment," Sam says, placing one arm out to block Rahzy from going any further.

Sammy and the Mantis walk just outside of the venue doors, conversing amongst themselves. Whatever is being said is inaudible to those inside.

Once in a safe, neutral distance in the street, Sam exhales, "So, tell me more."

Chapter 8

MATHIAS - FETELA

AT THE TOP OF THE DROP TOWER, STANDING CENTRIC OF Fetela, Mathias sits in a plush chair inside of his makeshift room, near one of the windows. He gazes out beyond the borders of his city into the Pines, viewing the faint lights from the outskirts.

Noticing his reflection in the glass, he examines his face. He reviews some of the scars he has received from various encounters in the desert. Mathias can almost remember how he received every one of them.

Shaking his head in irritation, he replays the recent conversation he had with The Guardian. But then, he gets distracted. "The sky is changing," he says, getting more comfortable in his chair.

"Just another cycle. Come to bed, baby," one of two women in the room says to him affectionately. One tall and slender woman lies on her back, perched against the headboard of the bed. She sips wine out of a small glass cup. She has perky breasts and a wide tattoo that covers most of her upper chest. Another woman is lying draped across the end of the bed, moving her hand above a chess board on the floor. She's making the pieces move to various positions without touching them.

Requesting a moment to think, Mathias raises a finger to the woman, but says nothing. Leaning forward, he rests his arms on his legs. He begins to think aloud, almost as if he is actually talking to the women in the room. "What would bring that conniving, greedy . . . fool of a man out of those walls again? He never steps foot outside those gates, let alone comes to my border. And he has done so more than once now."

"Maybe he is in trouble," The same tattooed woman contributes to Mathias' thought process.

"Trouble." Mathias sucks his teeth, standing and pacing the room. "Any trouble in which he finds himself, he has caused. Why should I care?"

Sitting up on the bed, the woman says, "Did you not agree to make deals with him? Trouble for him could be trouble for you."

Mathias looks over his shoulder, sighing deeply. "The only reason I deal with him is because of his father. His father and my father had a relationship. I was just trying to keep with tradition."

"Not all traditions are good ones."

"Y'all talk too much." The second woman interjects sternly. The chess pieces she had suspended in the air dropped briskly. "I can't concentrate."

Mathias walks over to the second woman, kneeling near her. Looking at her fondly, he places his hand on a rook. He moves it to capture a pawn on the chess board, helping her checkmate her imaginary opponent. "At this point . . . it's not about what's going on with him. But finding out what's going on with these humans – that . . . that should be my focus."

Patting the bed with her hand softly, the first woman summons Mathias to join them. Mathias approaches her, leaning in to slowly kiss her before lying down.

Awaking later, Mathias notices the sky is oddly still dark. Puzzled, he stares out into the sky for a bit from his bed, before casually looking over to check on his lovers who are sound asleep next to him. He rubs the first woman on her breast sensually, causing the tattoo on her chest to animate on her skin.

Her tattoo is of a bird perched in a tree. When her skin is touched in a certain way, the bird leaps into the air. It flies around the tree gleefully, landing again but on a different branch.

Gradually, Mathias gets out of bed and walks back near the window. He revisits the same thoughts he had before as he begins to quietly get dressed.

"Where are you going?" one of the women says groggily, changing her position. She lays on her stomach, one arm dangling on the side of the bed.

"Business. Go back to sleep," Mathias replies. He continues to put on his normal outfit: durable, reinforced linen pants and a shirt with leather straps around his waist and shoulders. He holsters two side arms before putting on a thick, hooded cloak. The cloak changes colors as he moves past various objects in the room. "I will see you both later."

Making his way through a set of aged, layered doors – one of which read *Employees Only* - Mathias inhales and exhales deeply. The doors led to a winding staircase that wrapped around the column in which the tower stood. After casually walking down the stairs and looking about at the various activities, Mathias finally reaches the bottom.

Immediately, Mathias is greeted by a group of people of various looks and sizes. They all have a similar, uniformed appearance like that of Mathias. All of them have specific responsibilities that hold Fetela together.

"Security?" Mathias says, wasting no time to begin his audit. The only greeting he provides is a quick bow of the head to everyone.

Stepping forward, the head of security replies, "All points and perimeters are monitored. Nothing to report. Even at the highest point of the wheel, nothing can be seen that may appear as a threat. Everything seems normal."

Nodding at the update, Mathias continues. "Food?"

"Our crops are steady but dwindling. We have planned trades to increase our inventory. I have been told that we may have access to new seedlings," the agricultural staff member replies.

"Excellent. Environmental? Have you'll noticed the difference in the sky?" Mathias looks up.

"Yes. But what's going on is beyond our knowledge. We do predict another normal cycle sometime soon," another person says.

Mathias pauses, glancing at the sky again. "Keep me informed. Trading?"

A woman holding a clipboard scans her paperwork quickly. "Usual trades today."

"Thank you all." Mathias begins to walk away, when his trade advisor gently touches his shoulder. "Yes? What is it?"

Waiting a moment before speaking again and ensuring that everyone had left, the trade advisor replies, "I received a note from the carrier last night."

"A note?"

"Yes. The person of interest will be coming again for another special trade."

Crossing his arms, Mathias responds inquisitively, "Why didn't you notify me of this last night?"

"Well, Mathias – you were . . . preoccupied. I didn't want to disturb you."

Mathias grumbles something under his breath. "With something like this, you must. Always."

Nodding, the advisor walks away.

Sometime later, Mathias and his trade advisor, along with four guards, wait for the person of interest at a location previously known as the funhouse. Many of the attractions at Fetela had been reconverted to businesses or living quarters. The funhouse was the only dwelling that was not completely repurposed. It now mostly operates as a meeting place for Mathias and his counsel.

"Mathias, she is here," another guard walks into the funhouse entrance.

Waving his hand, Mathias signals the guard to allow the woman to enter. The guard nods at the nonverbal order and walks back to the entrance, opening one of the double doors. He sticks his head out and has a short, muffled conversation.

The sound of the woman's heels can be heard before she is seen, along with subtle whistling from some of Mathias' men, gawking at the sight of the always mysterious and sexy woman who only comes to trade . . . on her terms.

"Mathias," the woman says assertively, nodding as she greets the rest of the room. "Ladies. Gentlemen. And whatever you all are."

Grinning, Mathias crosses one of his legs, "You know . . . it would be great to know your name, since I was willing to share mine."

"As I told you before, for the sake of safety and privacy —"

"I find it interesting that you only find *your* end of our dealings important enough for privacy. I, too, operate at a certain level of discretion in my affairs." Mathias extends his hand toward a chair, motioning the woman to sit.

Acknowledging, the woman sits softly in the chair. She crosses her legs, showing off her muscular thighs. Her heeled boots extended to just below her knee. "Tell me, Mathias, do you know the names of all the people with whom you trade? Where they're from? How old they are? If they like women, men – both? Or another type? Do they drink ale or not drink ale?"

Innocently, the trade advisor looks away in response to the woman's comments. Meanwhile, some of the guards grow excited and raise an eyebrow.

Frustrated by the woman's tone at this point, Mathias forms his mouth to speak but is interrupted.

"Your business is to provide a service. A service that doesn't require names or personal details," the woman continues.

Clearing his throat, Mathias replies, "I will kindly ask you to not tell me what my role is here, especially since you need something from me. If you don't want to tell me your name – fine. But if not, I have the option to end all trading with you."

Tightening her lips, the woman adjusts her full-length jacket that had become slightly stuck beneath her. She forms her mouth to speak before she, too, is interrupted.

"Now that we have that out of the way," Mathias snaps his fingers, prompting his guards to leave the room. Only his trade advisor remains, standing behind him with the nameless woman still sitting at attention. "Tell me what you are doing with the humans that we gave you."

"Why are you all of a sudden interested in what happens with our transactions once they are completed?"

Leaning forward in the aging chair, Mathias stares directly into the woman's eyes. "*What* . . . are you doing with the humans?"

The woman sighs deeply.

"I have people showing up to my borders asking about these humans. I advise you –"

"Oh, so you're advising me now?" The woman leans forward, almost mimicking Mathias' body language.

"I *advise* you to be a bit transparent, or our dealings are done."

Sitting back in her chair, the woman studies Mathias for a moment. She lets out an animated laugh before speaking again. "You know what I think? You don't have any more humans to trade."

Mathias looks away briefly. "The status of my inventory is irrelevant. Now. Answer my question."

The woman laughs again, but this time she's a bit nervous.

Standing, Mathias signals his guards to reenter the room.

"Okay. Wait." Raising one of her hands, the woman crosses her arms frustratingly. "How about I show you? It's . . . it's easier to explain what we do at my home in person."

Mathias studies the woman briefly before glancing over his shoulder at his trade advisor. The advisor shrugs a bit.

"Well then. Let's go now," Mathias responds after thinking about the offer briefly.

"We can't go now," the woman replies. "I need to brief my superiors and tell them that you will be visiting. Showing up without an invite, especially one in which they haven't approved, would not have good results - for you or for me. You can understand that, right?"

After the recent, unannounced visit by The Guardian, Mathias relates all too well to her sentiments. He nods in agreement.

Gathering her things, the woman says, "Give me a few night's rest. Then, I will meet you in the flatlands and take you there."

"How will we find you?"

"I will find you."

Nodding, Mathias watches as the woman stands and walks out of the funhouse. She is then escorted to the well-guarded gate near the boardwalk entrance and is granted access to leave. Slowly walking across the sand, her shapely silhouette slowly vanishes.

"I don't trust her," one of the guards says to no one in particular.

Mathias sighs. "Me neither, but damn she is sexy," he says as he walks away with his team of advisors with him. "Let's prepare."

Walking alone for some time before meeting up with more people from her entourage, the woman known for her vastly specific trade requests journeyed to the remote, agreed-upon location to reassemble. At this point, she connected with others and continued her journey to her home base. She travelled by a carriage that was pulled by four creatures with horse-like features.

Inside the carriage, she is kept company by two others. The first, a small, aging woman with long, bronzed hair, has eyes so light that they seem clear. This aging woman wears similar, but more aged-appropriate garments than her counterpart. The second person is a younger man that looks as if he could be the older woman's son because of their shared likeness. He has similar eyes and cheek bones, with a slim stature.

"So?" the man asks. As he awaits an answer to his question, he watches a small scorpion walk slowly around the shape of his hand.

"Mathias has grown suspicious of our trades."

"Suspicious? Why?" The old woman leans forward. "Is our end of the deal not sufficient? What has happened?"

"It seems that a third party has questioned him. It has caused him to withhold future trading until –"

"A third party? Who?" the old woman asks.

"Withhold future trading?" The young man slides forward in his seat, tossing the scorpion out of the window of the carriage. "Hakra will not be pleased with this, Feeza!"

Sighing deeply, Feeza casually moves her gaze from the man to outside of the carriage and crosses her legs. "Let me deal with Hakra. We must stay the course. This is only a slight hiccup."

"*Slight hiccup*," the man scoffs, shaking his head.

Chapter 9

THE ESCAPE – DELRUSIA ISLAND

THE SKY HAS DARKENED MORE OVER DELRUSIA ISLAND, making the surroundings a lot creepier than what it normally is. Extending as far as Kinth can see, the darkness brings challenges for him and the others as they walk toward the columned path. Slowing his pace and weary from the battle, Kinth takes his time; mostly because he is still carrying his father's body.

Distracted, he stands for a moment – almost statuesque. He looks up and notices the small specs of lights that seem to flicker behind the thick clouds. His concentration is broken, however, when Sir Grace whistles loudly. The odd-looking warden whistles multiple times, the last one being even louder than the times before it.

Awakening the winged-creature who had been resting in a cave away in the distance, the whistles are a signal to the beast to return to the island.

"Till we meet again!" Sir Grace says, laughing as he runs away.

A loud screech travels through the area swiftly, startling almost all the escaping prisoners. The wind around the island stirs more, causing loose particles from the prison structure to move considerably. Stones fall from the already wobbly platform. The columns leading to the prison sway subtly, as the fog thickens.

Various prisoners, some already making their way across the columns, stop and examine the sky. They begin to point at the creature. Many are shouting their concerns to one another as the winged-beast approaches. Some begin to turn around to attempt making it back inside the prison.

Swooping downward, the creature grabs multiple prisoners within the clasp of it jaws, flying back into the air afterwards. In one bite, the bodies of these prisoners are torn apart and swallowed whole. As it roars, the creature looks below at the scattering people and contemplates the next course of its meal.

Watching the attack with a frown, Kinth breathes heavily as he studies what is an oddly familiar situation.

"What do we do?!" Enrico shouts.

"Everyone!" Aldo waves his hand, grabbing the attention of the other prisoners. "Combine your abilities! We must fight! We must get across!"

Several of the prisoners having yet to maneuver across the columns come close to one another. Those with similar abilities worked together to create a shield. Therefore, some of the others could get across the columns safely. Blocking the winged-creature from grabbing those underneath it, the shield temporarily provides a good layer of safety.

Some others use their abilities to disorient and slow down the creature, creating a strong wind which moves objects in its path. Several stones of all sizes move about in the air, all rapid enough to block the view of the creature annoying it.

"Go on ahead!" Kinth yells before waving his arm to get Aldo's attention. "Aldo!"

Running towards him, Aldo ducks and rolls to avoid the large teeth of the creature and falling debris. Aldo is so close to the winged-beast that he can feel the breath of the creature on his neck.

"Here. Please take him up the path. I will distract the beast," Kinth says, a calmness in his voice that seemed strange for the event happening around him. He gently let his father's body slide down his arm and into the hands of Aldo.

Without saying anything in return, Aldo nods and quickly turns in the direction of the columns. He runs toward them, traversing the small round platforms under the dwindling layer of shields the other prisoners still manage to create.

At this moment, Kinth breathes in deeply. He releases a howl so loud and thunderous that, not only does it distract the beast, but the diminishing foundation of the prison begins to crack. The sound causes Aldo to stop also, almost missing a step. He then turns to see what animal was producing this sound.

"Go!" Kinth shouts, before howling again. Looking up at the creature, he shouts once more, "Come at me, you ugly piece of shit! Me! Right here!"

Changing its course, the creature hovers in the air several yards above the prison platform and columns. Its large wings move heavily, causing the sand and debris to move around the area. This thick layer blinds some of the prisoners, which causes them to fall from the columns.

"Hurry! Hurry!" Enrico screams, holding out his hand. He assists the remaining prisoners to get to the staircase on the other end of the columned path.

Another prisoner uses his ability to control the wind, moving and dividing the blinding fog and layer of sand from their path. Therefore, they are able to get across. Kinth continues to howl, screaming to keep the attention of the creature.

Aggressively, the creature darts further into the air, flying in circles a few times before nose-diving down toward Kinth. At the very last second possible, Kinth jumps out of the way and causes the beast to slam into the platform. A large chunk of the platform breaks off, causing the prison to further crumble on one side. Prisoners who remained in their cells began to scream as they held onto whatever they could to keep from falling.

"C'mon! That's all you got?!" Kinth shouts.

"Kinth! No!" Aldo screams, nearing the edge where Enrico stands.

Flying away, the creature turns around abruptly once it reaches a certain distance near other mountains. It hovers again, squinting its creepy eyes. The clouds hide some of its body, allowing the beast to quietly watch without being seen. Circling once more, it builds its momentum and dives toward Kinth again, who is becoming surrounded by the falling debris from the mangled prison walls.

Leaping into the air at a well-timed moment, Kinth jumps onto the creature's back, but then he almost falls off as the creature jerks erratically. It flies down further into the depths that Kinth once fell into himself some time ago. Continuing to move rapidly, the creature tries to shake Kinth off. Though, he fails because of the strong grasp Kinth has on its rugged skin in which he uses like a rein.

Yanking on the creature's skin, Kinth begins to force it to fly the course of his choosing. He yanks up, left and right. After some rebellion, the creature eventually subdues to the course of Kinth's choosing. But then, he spirals aimlessly. It does its best to shake Kinth from off of its back.

Amidst of this event, the prisoners have climbed the staircase. Most are at the edge of the escarpment, helping the others nearing the top. Some watch in awe as Kinth rides the winged-creature, a sight that is amazing to see, even for this group of odd individuals with peculiar pasts. Some even begin to cheer as they watch Kinth wrangle the beast in an apparent mid-air rodeo.

"C'mon, you foul-smelling, disgusting shit," Kinth mumbles under his breath, jerking and pulling on the creature. He keeps close to the creature's body, riding it up and down the immediate area around the prison.

In one last desperate attempt, Kinth uses all the strength he has left in his exhausted body, as he jams his hand into the back of the creature's head. Groaning, Kinth's face tightens because of the pain from the jagged, rough skin and bone of the creature. The texture had ripped off some of the skin from Kinth's hand and forearm. Removing his hand rapidly, he yanks a bloody mush from inside of the creature's head.

Shrieking in anguish, the beast jerks more. He briefly turns its head to bite at Kinth's leg. It continues to shriek, flying wildly before slowing down its pace through the air. Its wings stop flapping just over the platform of the prison, alerting Kinth that the creature was on course to smash directly into the escarpment.

"Oh no! NO! NO! NO!" Kinth stammers, yanking and pulling the beast upward.

The creature releases one final breath before its head falls and its wings droop, both dangling to its sides. Blood and saliva fall from its dying mouth. Dropping at a high speed, it crashes body first into the escarpment. The crash causes prisoners who had not been standing back far enough to fall. At the same time, Kinth leaps from the back of the beast, almost falling himself - latching onto one of the jagged edges of a stone.

Looking below his hanging body, Kinth watches as the creature tumbles against the rocks before falling into the depths of foggy darkness. Breathing heavily, Kinth scales the escarpment wall slowly toward the top; like the time he went rock climbing as a kid. "Hey! Somebody give me a hand!" His arms begin to tire.

Rushing over, one prisoner slides toward the edge of the cliff. He drops on his chest and reaches over to assist. Grabbing Kinth's extended hand, the prisoner realizes that he isn't strong enough by himself to assist Kinth the rest of the way.

"Shit! I can't – can't! One of y'all help me! This guy is massive!" the prisoner shouts. Some of the stone underneath Kinth's feet begins to crumble. "C'mon, man! Push with your feet!"

Sighing, Kinth says, "I'm . . . I'm exhausted."

Several more from the group run over and grab on to one another. The strongest of them assists by grabbing Kinth by his other arm just before Kinth loses his grip.

"Pull!" The prisoner shouts.

With one collective motion, the group of weary prisoners pull Kinth to the edge. Most of them drop to their knees and backsides, exhausted as well. They watch as their new, large savior climbs the rest of the way. Kinth lies on his back, doing his best to catch his breath.

Kinth struggles a bit while sitting up in order to kneel on one knee. Noticing, Enrico comes to help him up. Once to his feet, Kinth sighs as he studies the bewildered but thankful faces. Without saying anything, one of the smaller prisoners moves from behind a wall of onlookers and approaches Kinth. Saying nothing, he begins to wrap Kinth's arm and hand with a garment. Once finished, he extends his own hand. Kinth extends his in return, and the two shake. Several other prisoners follow suit, patting Kinth on the back, thankfully.

After a moment of solidarity, most of the prisoners begin to walk the path leading away from where Delrusia Island once stood. Kinth walks over to Aldo, who has been watching over Kinth's father. He rested the elderly man's body across a weathered strip of stone. Rubbing his father's brow, Kinth whispers something into his ear after kissing the side of his face.

"I'm sorry for your loss, friend," Aldo says after placing his hand on Kinth's shoulder. He then looks over his shoulder, noticing that Enrico and a handful of other prisoners are approaching.

"I – I can't even begin to thank you for freeing us. I owe you a great debt," Enrico says.

Slowly sitting next to his father, Kinth sighs, "I didn't free you, friend. If anything . . . I just motivated you. You freed yourself."

"What's next?" Aldo asks. "We need to get movin'. Who knows what else is out here waiting on us."

A young man stepped forward. "We wish to go with you, too. Wherever it is that you plan to travel."

All eyes are now on Kinth.

"Why y'all lookin' at me?" Kinth shifts his position, leaning forward on his knees. "You're free! Go! Find food! Find your families."

"This is my family now. I don't have nobody else. I'm not even sure how long I have been gone. I can't imagine my people still being around," the young man replies.

Glancing over at the remains of the island, Kinth says, "Anything is possible."

Enrico steps closer to Kinth and kneels, leaning in to whisper. "Most of these people have been stripped from their families. Who knows where they are now? Most of us are very weak. Let us come with you. We are all better off together."

"I agree with him," Aldo interjects. "Let 'em just roll with us to the nearest city at least."

Exhaling deeply before standing, Kinth rubs his eyes stressfully. "Doesn't seem like I have a choice, now does it?"

The group releases a collective sigh of relief.

The road is a long and unsettling for the group. Most of the prisoners were fed next to nothing while on the island. Now, they have absolutely nothing during their travels. The only food fell with the rest of the island. Moreover, the surrounding areas near the path to the prison is even more desolate.

After some time, the group notices that the desert foliage has become a bit more plentiful. They now walk a new, adjacent path. On this path they discover a few small blackberry trees behind abandoned buildings, along with a small garden that had been picked over. A few squash and dates are left for scavenging. But with the size of the group, the amount of crops they can pick is minimal for their sustainment.

Several of the prisoners plop to the ground in exhaustion, leaning on one another for support.

"Kinth, where are we going?" Aldo whispers.

Kinth breathes deeply, his mind still racing. "Gotta find a good place to bury him."

"I hate to say it this way, but if we don't find food and water soon, your father won't be the only person we will be burying," Aldo says distinctly.

Kinth nods.

"How about we put him somewhere safe, and come back for him? We can't run the risk of crossing paths with that unruly type, lugging around –" Aldo continues.

"I got it!" Kinth stands. "I got it."

Aldo stammers over his words. "Okay. I'm just . . . I'm not trying to be insensitive."

Approaching, Enrico listens in on the developing plan.

Walking away, Kinth is visibly frustrated. Looking around the immediate area, he inspects one of the building entrances before pushing through a pile of debris. Inside, he tosses around boxes and soiled clothing, loud enough to be heard outside.

"What is he doing?" Enrico asks.

"I don't know," Aldo says, lowering his gaze. "Give him a moment."

Without saying anything, Kinth walks briskly from the empty building toward his father's body that had been resting near the garden. Softly, Kinth kneels down to lift his father with both of his arms. He looks at him as he walks back toward the building, carefully taking him inside. Moments later, he walks back outside. He begins to stack chunks of brick, stone, and debris in front of the entrance. Then, he attempts to make it look even more abandoned than it already did. Aldo and Enrico notice and quickly come to help.

The three move almost in unison, grabbing and stacking enough objects to completely hide the building's entrance. But in doing so, they create enough commotion that the noise travels to the ears of an unknown person nearby.

"What in the hell are y'all doing?!" a soft, woman's voice rings out. She and a tall creature with dark eyes and a long narrow face approach the group of strangers quietly.

Startled by the unexpected visit, Aldo turns around quickly. Enrico does the same. Kinth sort of glances over his shoulder, but keeps stacking things inside.

"We are minding our business," Kinth snaps back at the question.

"Well, I was minding mine until this. That building is not your business. I don't think my friend will like it when he returns home and can't get inside of his place. What are you doing in there?"

Turning around, Kinth walks slowly toward the woman, causing her to cautiously back away. Standing tall, the creature with her gradually moves in front of her.

"I need to borrow this place. Just for a little while. I – I apologize for my shortness."

"Borrow? I can't lend what don't belong to me," the woman replies.

Kinth moves in closer to the woman, only a foot away. Holding out the palms of his hands, he continues, "Please. One of us has passed during our journey. I just need somewhere to keep him while we search for food. Then I will return for him and remove him. I just don't want to leave him out in the open land for wild animals to get to him."

After scanning Kinth more, the woman replies, "Food? Is that all y'all need?"

Kinth nods. "Yes, ma'am."

"Well, shit. There is a pub right over those hills there!"

Kinth and the others turn and look up, noticing smoke rising from over the hills. Kinth continues to gaze in the same direction, noticing that the sky is becoming rapidly darker than usual.

"We – we don't have much. Do you have anything we can trade for the food there?""

"Sorry, dear. You're on your own at this point. I haven't been in that place in many cycles. My boobs sat a little higher the last time I saw the inside of that place. But you need to hurry on, before my friend gets back. Eat and bring yo' ass right back and remove your friend," the woman says, moving her hand as she talks. She starts walking away before she finishes her train of thought.

"Okay, gents. You heard the woman. I guess - let's *hurry* up," Aldo says, walking through the group toward the hills.

Kinth hangs back for a moment. He studies the building as well as the woman as she and the creature walk in another direction.

Realizing that she had more to say, the woman stops and turns around swiftly. "Oh, and by the way . . . !"

"Yeah?" Kinth says curiously.

"Be careful over there. Those people don't take kindly to strangers. You were worried about wild things finding your friend. Those wild things sometimes originate in that place," the woman adds.

HAKRA

"Understood."

Chapter 10

THE GUARDIAN & TEAM – FLATLANDS

THE GUARDIAN CONTINUES OVER THE HILLS, DETERMINEDLY reconnecting with his men, who had been sent ahead after the attack by the old woman and the surprise appearance by the Desert Dwellers. Upon reconnecting with his unit, The Guardian doesn't say much. Thus, he still continued walking silently. His unit follows behind him as The Guardian heads in the direction of soft lighting in the distance.

His busy mind mauls over the conversation he had with Kira not too long ago. He wonders if the information she gave him was accurate, but why would she lie to him? After all, she knows that he is the only person who can free her mother.

"Let's break ahead," he says, snapping out of his thoughts to point at a metal sign in front of him. The sign is mangled but he deciphers enough of it to understand that a town was nearby.

The group stumbles on a cluster of buildings stacked in the nook of one of the hills. The buildings are surrounded by opposite-facing row houses, with the entire town's layout constructed to form a triangle.

The tight-knit area is active, as if no one moving about had any concern regarding the various threats lurking on the other side of the hills. Not including the strangers walking beyond the mangled fencing that separates the area from the rest of the Pines.

"I know this place," one of the guard's says to no one in particular.

Looking over his shoulder, The Guardian cocks an eye at the guard. "Then point us to where we can get a tasty beverage. Put your weapons away and spread out." He covers his face a bit to hide his identity.

A few blocks away, the group approach a three-story bar. People move about excitedly on each floor. While some of the patrons are drunk, they wander about the venue erratically. Some walk through the entrance, where they fight and fall into The Guardian's group. One patron in particular accidentally splashes ale onto The Guardian's face and clothing.

Quickly trying to dry The Guardian's clothing, this patron says apologetically, "Oh shit! I'm sorry!"

"Get away from me," The Guardian says, snatching the cloth from the man to wipe himself. He then turns his attention toward the steps leading into the bar.

Two large hybrid creatures are standing near the entrance talking to one another. After hearing the brief incident, they break their conversation. Both stare at the mysterious group of people walking towards them.

Their stares bring about an awkward silence.

"We don't want any trouble," one of the hybrids says as he slides out of the way. "Enjoy yourself."

The Guardian nods, stepping forward pass the pair casually. The group walks cautiously inside, inspecting every inch of the first level of the place. There is loud singing and conversations coming from various parts of the room. A small group is excitedly watching two women arm wrestle at one end of the bar.

"Everybody pick a spot and blend in. Just listen for now, See what you can find out. Reconnect out front," The Guardian whispers.

Dispersing in random directions, The Guardian's men heed to the orders. A few of them post up at the long, wooden bar on one side of the room. It's plagued with random dents, scratches, and holes, making it seem as if it was on its last leg. Some of the others join in on a poker game. There was a small stage in one corner with an aging three-piece drum set and an old piano. A woman sings softly, backed by the instruments in which she controlled telekinetically. A creature in the crowd, too, has joined in by blowing on his own horn-like contraption. A drunken man taps his leg, singing along as well.

A few of The Guardian's men go upstairs.

The Guardian himself strolls casually to another end of the bar, leaning on the rail as he watches his unit move about. He raises one of his fingers. After a moment, a shapely woman with dark, greenish skin walks over. She is wearing sunglasses and neck-rings, and has striking white hair which is braided into two ponytails. Her layered neck-rings seem to glow randomly, almost blinding at times.

"What can I get ya?" the woman asks.

Sizing the woman up, The Guardian then examines the other patrons at the bar.

"Let me know when you're ready," the woman impatiently begins to walk away.

"I apologize. But it's been a while since I have been to a place like this. I haven't seen a face as beautiful as yours."

Rolling her eyes, the woman shifts her weight onto one leg and crosses her arms. "What do you want, man? I'm too busy for this shit."

"I heard y'all have ale."

"What type do you want?"

"Something that has a bite to it," The Guardian says, biting at the air while snickering.

Shaking her head, the woman turns around. She speaks to some other people before grabbing a tall bottle from a shelf on the bottle rack. The bottle seems to be red, but it's actually the contents of the bottle causing the color of the bottle to change. She pours enough of the ale into a masonry glass to fill it a little less than halfway. Then, she slides it in front of The Guardian.

Other patrons close to the bar take notice at the glass sliding down the bar and raise their brows.

The Guardian lifts and examines the glass, smelling the ale deeply. He chuckles to himself, because the ale doesn't give off much of an odor. "Damn! That's it? Is this spicy, like you?" He leans in toward the woman, close enough to where the two could practically kiss.

Leaning in the same way, the woman stares directly into The Guardian's eyes. "If I didn't deliver on my promises, this bar would be empty. Now wouldn't it?"

"Hmph." The Guardian smells the ale once more, before slowly putting the tip of the glass to his lips. With a quick motion, he lifts the glass and takes one big gulp. Removing the glass from his mouth, he looks at the remaining ale and smiles smugly. "That's it? That was nothing. Seems your promises -"

The Guardian interrupts his own statement with one final sip. The woman leans on the bar, raising both eyebrows. She waits patiently as The Guardian finishes the remaining ale in his glass.

Dropping his glass, The Guardian steps backwards away from the bar. He begins to cough uncontrollably, grabbing at his chest. "What the – what the hell was in that?!"

The patrons begin to laugh crazily.

"You bite at me, I bite you back," the woman says, chuckling.

Waving his finger at the woman, The Guardian continues to cough. He steps backwards a little too far, falling into a chair that is positioned by a small table in a dark corner of the room. Bumping the table, he almost knocks over a glass that didn't belong to him.

"Easy, newcomer. I've traveled quite a ways for what's in that glass," the voice of a male stranger, sitting in the shadows, says. Only the glowing green of his eyes could be seen. He shuffles cards with his hands inside of leather gloves, flipping one over and placing the cards strategically in one row of seven.

The Guardian manages to control his cough, chuckling at how much of a fool he looked a moment ago. "Apologies. Seems I have underestimated the quality of the ale at this fine establishment."

"Seems so."

"Frank," The Guardian says, extending his hand.

The person in the shadows also extends their hand. "Pleasure to meet you, Frank."

"No name?"

"Names aren't that important in this place, which tells me you have never been here before. And looking at how you're dressed, you must be hunting for something."

HAKRA

The Guardian quickly looks down at his clothing, chuckling, "No, no. Nothing like that. You're pretty good at this game, huh?"

"I do okay. Just something to pass the time."

"Well, I'm good at finding things. But I've been having a little trouble lately finding what I'm searching for."

Continuing to flip cards, the person says, "And that would be?"

"A few people from my city have gone missing," The Guardian adjusts himself in his seat.

The man continues to flip over cards, moving them around on the table strategically to match suits and organize them numerically.

"Have you seen anything odd since you been here?" The Guardian continues.

Leaning forward on the table, the man brings his face into the light. He has the cheeks and chin of a fit, human man. But he has the nose, eyes, and forehead of something aquatic. Attached to his head are tentacles that hang like thick locks of hair. "With the exception of this ole mug, and everyone else that walks in this place — no. No, I have not seen anything . . . *odd*," he says, laughing boisterously.

"Seems we have something in common," The Guardian says, turning his body to face the man and joining in on the laughter.

"Oh yeah? And what would that be?"

Leaning on the table in a similar fashion, The Guardian rolls up one of his sleeves and begins to mutate into a mantis. His eyes begin to change colors and the shape of his face changes gradually.

"What a nice trick."

The Guardian scoffs.

"So, I am supposed to do what – exactly - after seeing that?"

"You are a functioning hybrid, like me. We are alike. We should be helping each other out," The Guardian says, pleading.

Shuffling a card fancily with one hand, the aquatic man replies, "Alike? You hide behind a human's face. I have accepted who I am many cycles ago. I am proud to be of Cepha."

Sighing, The Guardian leans back in his seat.

"You tell me your story and I will tell you what I know about *missing* people," the man adds.

"My story? Look, man – I'm as simple as anyone else in this joint."

"Don't bullshit me. I saw you and your men when you walked in. You honestly think that some of these people wouldn't recognize your face from those crappy flyers floating around Hock City?"

A bit stunned from the man's comments, The Guardian doesn't respond.

"Yeah. I know who you are, your highness. Now. Tell me your story."

"My story? About what? I oversee Hock City. I –"

"No, no, no." The man points at his own face. "I want to know about how you became like this."

Exhaling, The Guardian crosses one of his legs over the other. Stroking his chin, he looks around the room for a moment before responding. "When the event happened, I was very young. I was . . . fond of insects. I had a pet spider and, at one point, I also had some other stuff. Kid shit. But after my spider got loose, my father wouldn't get me another. Told me that there were plenty spiders in the wild that I could play with. Plus, my mother didn't like the spider. So, eventually, I found a new pet. A mantis."

"And you were with this mantis when the event happened?"

"Pretty much. It stayed with me in my room," The Guardian begins to fiddle with a stack of poker chips on the table. "I never told anyone that story. Only those who were there, know. Until now."

Without notice, some of The Guardian's men approach the table quietly. Two of them turn to face the crowd, blocking the table from the view of others, while others lean in and whisper something in The Guardian's ear.

After he nods, The Guardian stands. "My apologies, but I must be on my way. It was a pleasure."

"So soon? And we were just starting to get to know one another."

"Another time, friend," The Guardian nods, walking away briskly. "I'm sure with a face like that, we will meet again."

The bartending woman had been listening to some of the conversation while making her rounds, watching from various points of the bar. She notices The Guardian leaving. "Hey! Hey! You owe me for that drink!"

The Guardian pauses, snapping his finger to one of his men. The guard walks over to the bar and retrieves his bag from his back. Reaching inside, he pulls out something and hands it to the woman. Then, he returns to the group.

Outside of the venue, The Guardian and his men regroup. Standing several feet away from the entrance, they wait for each member to report and prepare to travel again.

"What was learned? Anything useful?" The Guardian asks.

"Sir, I . . . I –"

"Well? Spit it out!"

"I bedded a woman while inside."

The other soldiers begin to chuckle and praise the news amongst themselves.

"About time!" one of the men sings, laughingly. "But man that was quick!"

"Yeah! He must be . . . quick . . . at the draw!"

Energetic laughter continues.

"Shut the hell up!" the guard that shared the news replies.

The Guardian sighs, "Alright. Alright. Quiet down, please. Why do you feel the need to tell me that you bedded a woman?"

"The woman told me some things that may relate to your search," the soldier approaches, whispering some information.

"Really, now? Go on."

A couple of floors above them, the Cepha man remains in the shadows, gently lifting the nearby window with one finger. The window is lifted only enough to listen to the conversation happening outside. Although a bit muffled, he hears all that he must.

"The woman said that, at various times, people from a city in which she used to live would randomly go missing. The rumor was that the people were being kidnapped. They were being taken to an old medical facility - that way," the guard adds, pointing. "But most people never believed it. Like an urban legend. They just assumed that people moved on or died during their journeys."

Crossing his arms, The Guardian glances in the direction the guard had been pointing, "What is this city that this happened in?"

"Longleaf."

"Do you trust this information?" The Guardian asks.

"Well, she was very, um . . . free - because of the ale. She definitely could throw 'em back. So, yes. Yes I do."

"Hmm. I am no stranger to drunken confessions. Let's find somewhere to lie our heads. We will reconvene our travels when rested."

Back inside the bar, the Cepha man curses under his breath, quickly grabbing his things to leave out of the rear exit.

Chapter 11

LANGSTON, JESSE & WINSTON – BIYO BRIDGE

STARING AT THE MANGLED, DANGLING SIGN, Langston, Jesse and Winston ponder on which way to go. From what they can make out, there are at least four places scribbled on the sign. Although, most of the wording is illegible.

"So, which way?" Jesse asks again. He attempts to mouth possible words to himself to make sense of the sign.

Langston paces, inspecting the sign, while also examining the fork in the bridge. Both directions look exactly the same. Jesse does his best to reposition the sign in its original formation, but hasn't any luck. Falling again, the sign smacks him on the arm.

"Well, which way?" Langston says eagerly, approaching Winston.

Placing one hand over his mouth, Winston approaches the sign and touches it softly. Pondering, he looks in both directions and closes his eyes. After a moment, he begins to walk slowly. "I believe this is the way."

"Are you sure? Hey!" Langston says, trotting behind him. "Wait up!"

Jesse has become predisposed with the environment. Both paths look the same but feel more eerie to him, causing his delay in following the others. The wind and condensation creates a soft, but menacing sound to his ears. Misty wind creates chills that run through his body.

"Jesse! C'mon!"

"I apologize, young Langston. But I . . . I am low on energy. But I do believe we are on the right course." Winston uses a cloth to wipe his brow.

"Do you need to rest?"

Breathing deeply, Winston sighs after he looks at the path in front of him. "Yes. I think that would be wise."

The two take a breather. Sitting on the bridge, they rest their backs on columns across from one another.

"My abilities take a lot out of me. I forget that I am no longer the young man I once was."

"I don't understand when you say that . . . I thought your abilities helped you," Langston says.

"There is more I must tell you. What I have to say may be troublesome to you, but it needs to be said nonetheless."

"Troublesome?" Langston repositions himself, propping up one knee.

Moving in closer, Jesse sits slightly between the two.

"This actually pertains to you more, Jesse."

"Me?"

"Yes. I guess this is a good time to continue where we left off in my story; sort of. A very long time ago, the original Guardian started to notice that our abilities were not only helping us, as you say Langston, but also working against us."

"Working against you? How?" Langston asks.

"Well, there is no easy way to answer that. Or one way. But The Guardian believed that our abilities were aging us rapidly. For some of us, it took our already troubled bodies and caused our ailments to worsen. At first, I didn't quite understand his theory, nor believed it. Still, I opened my mind to the opinion when I noticed the people around us."

"What about the people?"

"Well, some became sluggish. They would get tired faster from doing basic things that they were used to doing. Including me. I had a lot more energy and was much livelier. But the more I used my abilities, the more exhaustion I felt. Then, eventually I started to gray – well before the time I believe I should have started graying." Stroking his beard, Winston pauses before standing. He readies himself to continue the journey. Stretching his body from side to side, he begins to stroll in the same direction as previously.

"Are you sure you're ready to continue?" Langston asks.

"Yes, yes. Just talking about this is – making me . . . let's just continue." The old man shakes his head, taking a moment to readjust his thoughts. Langston and Jesse gather themselves to follow him. Once the three are back in stride, the old man continues. "This ole beard you see was once quite thick and black."

Interrupting anxiously, Jesse says, "So what did The Guardian do to help the people?"

"Well, that is the unfortunate part. The Guardian had regular meetings with his counsel where I was a member. We were a group of advisors, and I helped him lead the city as best as we could. He was ready to present his theories and ideas of a solution but it was too late."

"Too late?" Jesse looks up at Winston.

"Yes. Yes. The Guardian was dethroned by his own son. Thereafter, his theories disappeared just as he did."

A quiet falls amongst the three, as everyone takes a moment to reflect on the words shared.

"So does this mean I will die because of my gifts?" Jesse asks, worriedly.

Stopping suddenly, Winston looks at Jesse tenderly. He kneels down and places his hand on the boy's shoulder. "We must all die someday. But not today, young Jesse. And not any time soon."

"We need to let as many as possible know this!" Langston interrupts.

Standing upright again, Winston holds his chin with his thumb and index finger. "Know what?"

"The true Guardian's theories."

"Ha! That sounds like quite the task for just three people – one of them being an old snail." Winston chuckles.

"There's gotta be a way."

Little did the three know at the moment, but the more that they talked, the further they seemed to have traveled. But Winston's story time had been interrupted by Jesse. He had managed to get a ways ahead of the other two.

"Look!" Jesse shouts, pointing.

The group had finally reached the end of the bridged path, nearing a hill. At the apex of the hill, Jesse could see a small group of people walking. Throwing caution to the wind, Jesse bolted toward the people.

"Jesse! Jesse! Wait a minute!" Langston took off behind him.

Snickering at the act, Winston waved at the two, "Don't mind me, I will catch up!"

Upon reaching the small group of people, Jesse wastes no time with his inquiries. "Hey! Where are you guys going?"

A few of the people within the group glance at Jesse, but do not respond.

Growing even more inquisitive, Jesse says, "My friends and I are hungry. Can you tell us where we can find any food?"

A creature within the group, who wore a large blanket and goggles, approaches Jesse quietly but said nothing. Upon reaching Jesse, it placed one hand over its mouth and then pointed in another direction with the other.

Nodding, Jesse looks beyond the stretch of the creature's arm and notices more movement.

"Jesse! Man, you can't run ahead like that," Langston says, catching up.

"Mr. Langston, look," Jesse replies, quietly.

Langston notices both groups of people, near and far.

"They said there is food that way."

Finally catching up to the others, the old man is briefed on the same information as Langston. The three weary travelers follow behind the group of creatures but at a distance. It seems the group is traveling in the same direction. After walking for a ways up and down a hill and around a bend, the three approach a small section of buildings.

Winston is surprised at the layout of the area. The buildings are familiar to him, partly because they have a similar design as the row houses in the front section of the neighborhood where he lives. The sand is so heavy and thick. It seems as if the buildings were trying to escape from it, protruding from the hardened soil and rock. Mounds of debris are immersed in the softer sand on the sides and in front, protruding in a similar fashion. This gives off the essence of abstract statues that would appear in a museum.

Some of the buried items included: a motorcycle, with only its backend showing, the limbs of a mangled mannequin, wooden doors, poles and more.

Interrupting the three followers, the creature whom provided silent instructions approaches Jesse again. As before, the creature doesn't say a word. Rather, he points to a building across the street from where they are standing.

"Okay! Thank you!" Jesse says after cocking his head to the side to see around the tall creature. He turns his attention to Langston and Winston, who were preoccupied with examining the area. "He said we can eat over there."

"Well then, let's go. So I can rest my weary feet," Winston says.

Crossing the dusty, sand-stricken street, Langston leads the way toward the building. There are no signs or activity near the front entrance, with the exception of various patrons randomly leaving or entering the business. Nor much sound. For this being a place to break bread and drink, it was awfully quiet outside.

"You sure this is the place?" Langston says after stopping at the curb, just in front of the building's entrance.

Jesse shrugs. "This is where he pointed."

"We'll be fine," Winston adds, scooting his way between the two. "It looks like it might be a hostel, which for us is great news."

Pushing through two wooden doors, Winston walks inside the bar and quickly scans the room. The bar is quite rustic and bare, having makeshift tables made out of the remains of old dressers and bookshelves; refrigerators and metal scraps. Slabs of oddly shaped meat hang in a row on one side of the room. A creature throws various spices and grains on some of the meat, rubbing it harshly before tossing it in a large, rectangular tub with a fire burning beneath it.

At the various tables are patrons; mostly hybrid creatures, beasts and a few who look almost human. A very pale man with red eyes tends to those at a bar, moving rapidly up and down one side of the room. More than once, a waitress appears to almost run into the bartender. But like an orchestrated dance, they quickly avoid a collision.

The wooden doors slam behind Jesse, causing the room to quiet more than what it already was. Everyone diverts their attention briefly to the newcomers, sending deep and piercing stares. But after this brief moment, they continue to eat, drink and converse with each other.

"Whew. Damn, Jesse," Langston sighs, startled.

"Sorry."

"Ha! Relax, my young friend. We are amongst friends!" Winston says.

Langston glances at Winston and then back at the room. "Doesn't seem too friendly."

Sitting down at one of the partially empty tables, Winston uses his abilities to review the thoughts and behavior in the room. Most of the patrons are from Hock City, having made their way this far to avoid the threats of staying near the city during the evacuation. Some of the other patrons were regular wanderers; nomadic people from the flatlands and other areas. Many of the thoughts of these people were filled with anxiety and stress.

"You don't have to do that. You can just ask me what you wanna know. It's safe in here." A soft, but stern, womanly voice breaks Winston's concentration. The approaching woman is one of the bar's waitresses. She wears baggy pants, a tank top and wide googles on her forehead.

"Oh my. I did not mean to offend, young lady. A creature of habit," Winston says.

"You aren't the only person who can do that," the waitress adds. "Everyone in here probably can do something. But we leave what we can do out there and not in here."

"I don't understand," Jesse asks.

The waitress smiles and comes around the table. She kneels to meet Jesse at eye level. "Consider this a safe place. The people you see in here may look scary. They may have special things they can do, but they only use their scary looks and special things out there," she adds, pointing toward the door.

"Oh . . . okay." Hypnotized by the woman's oddly pleasant smell, Jesse's response is almost robotic.

Chuckling, the waitress stands. "Now, what can I get y'all?"

"Whatever food you have will do us fine," Winston responds.

"Well, all we have that seems to stretch is soup. It's made from the finest we could find in the wild outside those doors."

Jesse practically cuts the woman off before she can finish her sentence. "Soup is good."

The waitress nods. "Okay, baby. I will bring y'all some tea, too. Doesn't look like y'all need any adult beverages. Especially you." She laughs as she walks away. "And if you need some beds later, let me know. We have limited space upstairs. We normally save them for our older folk, women and children. At least y'all got two out of the three."

"Thank you kindly," Winston replies.

As the waitress makes her way through another set of doors to the kitchen, Langston notices that, just over her shoulder, a young woman is sitting in a back corner by herself. She's looking down at something. Even though she is not saying much, she's mouthing words to herself. Every so often, she is visited by the waitress and the two share a few laughs. The woman's smile does something to Langston. She looks strikingly familiar to him, so familiar in fact, that he finds himself caught in a daze.

"Mr. Langston. Mr. Langstonnnn!" Jesse sings, shoving his leg to get his attention.

"Sorry."

"Are you okay, my boy?" The old man leans forward on the table, patting Langston's hand.

"Yeah. I just – nothing. Never mind."

Langston begins to think quietly as the three wait:

Man, that sure looks like Talicia. But she wouldn't be here. Would she? Shit, I don't even know where I am. Damn. Could that be her? Sweet, sexy, Talicia.

At this very moment, the waitress returns – hearing Langston's thoughts. "How do you know Talicia?"

"Huh? Wait – that's not fair. Please don't do that. You just told us not to do that," Langston says, fumbling some over his words.

"I'm sorry. I know. But I heard you say her name, so I had to speak up. How do you know Talicia?!" Adrenaline begins to rush through the waitress's body, causing her tone to elevate. She ends up questioning Langston at an octave to cause a scene.

Perturbed, Langston nervously stands. "Jesse, Winston – lets go. Please."

"But we haven't eaten yet," Jesse pleads.

Winston smirks a bit, looking back and forth at Langston. The waitress and a woman that seems to be Talicia approaching.

As Langston and the waitress trade more words, the woman reaches them. She touches Langston gently on the arm before speaking softly, "Langston?"

Chapter 12

FEEZA & OTHERS - IFERA MEDICAL PARK

TROTTING STEADILY, THE SOUND OF THE HORSES MOVING across the sandy road, nearly imitating rainfall, has been soothing to the three travelers – if the Pines ever had consistent rain to enjoy. It has been many cycles since heavy moisture has fallen from the darkened sky, resulting from the climate-changing event that changed in addition to everything else. But the three travelers are used to this, making their way from Fetela back home.

The trots become sparse, as the carriage closes in on its destination. Muffled conversations by those up front controlling the beasts pulling the carriage grew louder.

Slowing down, the horse-like creatures neigh loudly. It's enough to wake the aging woman and her male counterpart, both who had been nodding for most of the ride. The aging woman nudges the young man a couple of times to alert him.

Feeza, though awake, has been pondering too many things to close an eye. Her only job was to make the necessary trades per the instructions of her superior. And, she has never returned home empty-handed. How would she explain this?

Staring at Feeza, as if she was reading her mind, the old woman says, "So, what will you be telling Hakra?"

"Not sure just yet. But let me worry about the dialogue. You do whatever you must do, old woman. I don't even know why he asked you two to join me this time," Feeza snaps back.

"We are here," The deep voice of a man enters the carriage from a small window positioned at the front. He holds the reins tightly, with large scaly hands – pulling back enough on them to cause the creatures to stop.

A long, barbed-wired fence sits in front of the carriage stands, positioned just behind mangled barrier walls. The fence appears to have been disguised underneath foliage that had been purposely placed atop of it. I BOW TO NO

ONE. NATURE IS MY ONLY MASTER, has been spray painted across the walls in large lettering closest to its entrance.

At each corner of the fencing stands several guards of both creature, hybrids and others whom look human but are not. Many of these guards are unarmed, with the exception of their various abilities. They pace the length of the barriers, watching out for threats.

At the center of the fence is one entrance, with a large sign above it that reads: IFERA MEDICAL PARK. At the core of this medical park is a tall, hospital-like facility. It had been vandalized numerous times by the looks of it before it was taken over by the current occupants.

The young man wipes off his clothing as he steps outside the carriage first. "I'm glad I don't have to make these trips with you regularly. Look at how filthy I have become," he says, holding the carriage door open for the others.

"Stop your whining and help me out," the old woman replies. Looking up, she notices how the sky changed more during their ride home. "Hmph. They must be testing a bit more than usual."

Following behind the two, Feeza steps outside the carriage, and exhales deeply to relax. She looks around the area, traversing her thoughts before taking one step closer to the main entrance.

"Well, after you," the man says. "Hope you are ready."

"Thanks for the vote of confidence, Niandres." Feeza rolls her eyes and begins to walk toward the barrier walls.

Leading the way, Feeza walks on the largest, centermost sidewalk. It's chipped and split in some areas, with dry, brown foliage piercing through some of the cracks. This sidewalk connects the large facility to other smaller, office buildings. At the end of this walkway stands the tall facility building. IFERA HOSPITAL is printed in block, bold lettering; still intact. Meanwhile, the rest of the area looks deserted and neglected. More armed guards stand waiting at each side of the building and entrance, and at various points on the roof.

The guards notice Feeza and the others approaching. Without saying a word, they open the facility's doors. Inside the facility are various floors and rooms, all dimly lit and some completely dark. As Feeza and the others walk the hall, various motion-censored lights activate. Soiled, aging gurneys and hospital beds sparsely line the walls in the various hallways.

At the end of this particular hallway are three wide elevators, but only one seems to be active. The administration floor, identified by an 'A,' is lighted. Feeza presses the button to call the elevator to the main floor. Still within her thoughts, she watches the elevator travel from A, 10, 9 – all of the way to the main floor in which she and the others await.

Dinging, the elevator button illuminates with an 'M' on the screen above the doors. Niandres walks in first, holding the door open for Feeza and then the aging woman. Standing against each of the walls, the three look at various points of the elevator as the doors closes and it begins to rise.

"This should be interesting," Niandres says, chuckling to himself.

Folding her arms, Feeza clears her throat.

"Nothing to say?"

"Oh, shut up, Niandres. Despite our differences, we can all be punished for our shortcomings . . . about this matter. So, please just - just be quiet," the aging woman interjects.

Niandres scoffs.

Dinging again, the elevator doors open to show an intersection of more dimly lit hallways. Lighting is somewhat unstable and flickers randomly. An unusual, repulsive smell fills the air. An odor accrued from the sick people that once occupied the facility.

Feeza walks by more security, pacing the hallway. She pushes through a set of doors that lead to an empty waiting area, with the exception of a woman behind a desk. Slow tempo electro-jazz music plays from a speaker in the ceiling. At the desk, the woman glances downward as she reads an old magazine.

"We need to see him," Feeza says, walking aggressively toward another set of double-doors.

"Wait, wait! I need to tell him! Wait!" The woman fumbles over her magazine as she tries to stop Feeza. "You can't just walk in like that!"

Hearing the secretary's cry, security runs toward the sound. Pushing by Niandres, they almost knock down the aging woman who was next to him. As they close in on the secretary, who is right on Feeza's coattail, Hakra's voice rings out, "It's all right. She can enter. Everyone else – out." The voice is deep, but calm – gentle but disturbing.

Backing out of the room quietly, the secretary quickly forces everyone else behind her to do the same and closes both doors. An eerie silence grows just after the doors latch together.

Feeza strokes her hands slowly, concerned of how her news would be received. She tries to speak a couple of times but her nervousness held back her words. "It was a long journey this . . . this time. At least it felt long."

"Is that right?" Hakra replies, his back turned. He looks out of one section of a large, panoramic window. He is tall; slender but with broad shoulders underneath a well-fitted hooded coat that extends to his feet. Most of his face is covered, with a scarf wrapped tightly around his lower face. He wears a mask made out of leather scraps wrapped around his eyes.

"Yes, I feel a bit drained. We, uh -"

"Drained? How so? Since you have returned empty-handed?"

Flustered, Feeza says, "I apologize, but we have a bit of a problem."

"A problem? I am not fond of these words."

"Please. Just listen. Mathias is questioning our trade requests. He wants to know more about what we are doing with our subjects."

"Why do I care what he wants after we close our deals?"

"I believe he no longer has the specific subjects that you need. His advisors must be in his ears about my visits."

"Well, find a new area to acquire the subjects we need."

"That's just it. We have looked all over these lands. Mathias was the only person left who had access to what you need. Now, it seems that he doesn't have any more."

Annoyed, Hakra turns around and sits on the edge of a long desk centered in front of the window. Just over his shoulder, the remnants of the landscape around the facility shine through the window. The sky is more complex from this view, since one particular mountain is not too far away. It looks almost as if the mountain peak was touching the sky.

Stepping forward, Feeza softens her voice. "When will I get to see your face?" She reaches out, attempting to touch the man affectionately.

"Why is my face so important to you?"

"You rescued me and I am forever grateful. I have been by your side, doing as you wish for as long as I can remember. I just want to see you . . . all of you. I want to kiss your face."

Titling his head, Hakra smiles behind his face covering. He approaches Feeza, gently touching her face with his hands that are covered by leather gloves.

Feeza practically melts from his touch, closing her eyes and moving her face against his fingers. In her mind, she pretends that she was feeling his skin versus the rough, worn leather.

"I told you, Feeza, that my skin is sensitive to the harsh climate in which we live in. One day, you will see my face. Until that day . . . my face is not important. But my orders – they are."

"I understand," Feeza sighs, feeling depleted. "There is one more thing."

"Which is?"

"I recommend that we expand our testing to other specimens."

Softening his tone, Hakra says, "Because of the dwindling numbers of our prime subjects?"

"Yes."

"Hmm. And with whom do you think we should start?"

"Mathias and his people. From what I can gather, he may have reliable hybrids in his midst," Feeza says, looking away.

"Hmm," Hakra folds his arms.

"There is something else. Mathias had many questions this time. Something has him on edge."

Stunned, Hakra says, "What could have him on edge?"

"I'm not sure. But he bombarded me with questions. To avoid exposing too much, I made an offer to him."

Returning to the window, Hakra gazes out at the surroundings. "An offer?"

"I told him that he could come and see what we are doing here. I . . . I guess I got panicked by his questions."

Turning around briskly, Hakra's tone hardens. "Feeza, the only reasons why I have allowed you to speak on my behalf is because you have shown on several occasions that you can make sound decisions. But this is not one of them! I have other things to focus on which keep me extremely busy."

"I know. I know. I'm sorry. I panicked."

"This place stands only because of a high level of discretion. We can't afford for anyone to know what we do here."

Rubbing her brow, Feeza replies, "Yes, I know. That's why we don't let him leave . . . when he comes."

"Don't let him leave? What are you getting at?"

"He either joins us or becomes a test subject. We take him, and then we take Fetela. And then any city near it."

Smiling, Hakra says nothing for a moment and studies Feeza's body language. Shocked by Feeza's words, he says, "Let's take a walk." He storms pass her, opening both double doors and walking through the waiting room. "You two, come with us," he says, speaking to the old woman and Niandres who had been on edge in the waiting room. "Lock up my quarters and ensure no one is allowed up." He orders the woman at the desk and the security nearby.

Walking down multiple hallways, the three follow their leader to another elevator that requires a special key. After inserting the key, Hakra turns it and presses a button. Once the elevator doors are activated, they open. The four individuals enter and begin to descend after Hakra presses the button for BL1, the first floor basement level of the facility.

After a short moment, the elevator slows and stops at this location. A long, dark corridor is revealed to them.

"After you," Hakra says quietly.

Feeza and the others hesitantly step out of the elevator, examining the darkness ahead of them.

"Sir, I'm sorry for my mistake. Please," Feeza pleads, her anxiety growing because of the quiet and Hakra's sudden change of demeanor.

The aging woman looks over at Niandres worriedly. "Whatever was done was not our doing. We waited for Feeza many yards away as she conducted your business. She didn't want us to join her."

"Yes! Exactly," Niandres nervously chimes in.

Gently shoving the three, Hakra says, "Just walk."

As the group walks the length of the hallway, motion-activated lights turn on. Strange, electrical sounds gradually grow clearer as the group approaches a wide, tinted glass door.

Feeza and the others step to the side as Hakra approaches a panel on the right side of the door. Approaching the door slowly, he looks over his shoulder before typing in six numbers on a keypad. The wide doors retract and the sounds inside become full to their ears.

In the next room, there is a mechanical, bridged walkway that leads to a round area of machinery. Various electrical wires, tubing and other connections drape the walls, the floors and the ceiling of the room. At the very center of this area is a tube filled with a variety of dark colors. It's large enough to fit multiple people, and extends in variations to the top of the room and through the ceiling.

Despite its cold appearance, the room is warm, mostly because of the various testing and equipment being used within it.

"Oh . . . oh my," Feeza is in awe. She steps closer to watch as several people wearing odd outfits covering their entire bodies move about.

"I never seen anything like this before," Niandres adds.

Bolting behind Feeza, Hakra grabs her throat and bends one of her arms behind her back. "This! This is why we must be careful! This! What you see here is my only reason for living! Do you understand?! Do you?!"

The old woman practically falls trying to move out of the way. She is too in shock to scream. Niandres moves behind one of the cabinets nearby.

"Yes! Yes!" Feeza says, pleading.

"Say you understand!"

Feeza screams, "I understand! Hakra! I understand!"

Sharply, Hakra releases his grasp from Feeza and walks to the edge of the pathway just before the testing area.

Feeza coughs aggressively.

"Now. Back to our problem at hand," Hakra says.

Chapter 13

KINTH & OTHERS – THE PUB

THE SKY HAS FURTHER DARKENED AND CHANGED, CAUSING the travel up and over the various hills to become troublesome. Kinth and the weary group of prisoners aren't too far away from the pub recommended by the local woman. But because of their exhaustion, it seems like it's taking forever to get there.

As they close in on the dwelling, the bunch examine the area just outside of it. It is a modest place of business, standing alone from the other nearby buildings. Most of the buildings are carved from the stone that has protruded from the side of the nearest mountain. Wooden columns border the building, along with matching stained-glass window coverings and doors.

Enrico approaches the large, wooden door, holding his ear close to it. Therefore, he could listen before entering. Calm, subtle conversations bounce from off the walls. Just as he reaches his hand to open one of the doors, it flies open. A handful of drunken creatures stumble onto the front walkway.

"Get outta our way, man! Gotta bullet in the chamber, ready to fly!" one of the creatures says before laughing. He yanks his buddy to one side of the building, pulling him behind a stack of trash bags. The others with them watch as the one creature leans forward, regurgitating everything it had consumed inside the venue.

Aldo also watches as he stands beside Kinth. Laughing at the spectacle, he whispers, "Seems like my kind of spot."

"Let's go in, before I change my mind about this place," Kinth scoffs.

One by one, the group falls into the venue almost unnoticed. They sit at the nearest picnic-style table, positioned in rows from the very front of the venue to the rear but on adjacent walls. The room is illuminated by candles strategically placed on the tables. They're installed in wide, cast-iron chandeliers.

Lining the back wall after the tables is a bar, positioned upon a platform. To the side of it is an average-sized wrestling pit. Bystanders enjoy other patrons who brawl for goods while consuming alcoholic beverages. Up for grabs are various weapons, clothing, food and more.

"Alright. So we here. How are we supposed to get something to drink with nothing to offer?" one of the prisoners says.

Kinth stands and takes a quick look around. "Hold that thought." Walking towards the bar in the back of the room, he bumps into a patron causing her to spill some of her drink.

"Hey!" the woman yelps.

Apologetically, Kinth replies, "Sorry about that."

Someone's hand slams onto Kinth's shoulder. "You bothering the lady?" A slightly drunken creature, with oversized teeth and a partly mangled mouth asks, squaring up for a brawl. It is about Kinth's size and height.

"No. Just a mild collision," Kinth replies with a calm tone. "So, take your hand off me."

"Well how about you *collide* with me in the ring?!" the creature says, pointing with his thumb. His statement is met with loud cheers of agreement by those nearby.

Kinth sighs, exhausted from the journey and even more exhausted by the violence from which he had just escaped. He begins to form a response when a small, but confident voice interjects.

"Nope! No, sir! My friend is not here for any of that. So move along!" The voice grows louder. Whomever it was has been moving in closer to the action.

Kinth begins to feel movement around him just before he gets jabbed in the side. Looking down, his eyebrows raise. "Miles?"

"The one and only, baby!"

"Hey, he's mine next, rodent!" The large creature reinserts himself into the conversation, batting his chest to intimidate those in the area.

"I don't wanna fight this guy, you idiot. Do you really think my small ass can – you know what? Never mind." Miles hops up onto the nearest table to be heard more by the room. "Listen, you will get a new opponent soon enough. But this guy is not here to fight! Capisce?!"

The creature grunts, looking at Kinth again before storming away. Other nearby patrons reconvene their drinking and conversations.

"Hey, barkeep. Get my friends some bread and ale!" Miles shouts over his shoulder.

"Miles, what are you doing here?" Kinth says, sitting down at the table upon which Miles stands. Aldo, Enrico, and a few of the other prisoners sit as well, having quietly come to Kinth's aid if necessary, during the brief standoff.

"First of all – who are these poor bastards you got with you? Sheesh! Looks like y'all been through hell and back! Barkeep! Hurry it up!"

Aldo chuckles, "That's one way of describing it."

"Kinth helped us escape the island," Enrico replies.

Beginning to pace, Miles says, "Island? What island?"

Placing both arms on the table, Kinth leans forward to whisper, "Miles. What are you doing here? You were supposed to be helping the kid and . . . the human. How did you know I would be here?"

"I did help them! I took Jesse and our new friend to your uncle's place. He had that pin you gave him and was adamant on going there. That was the last I'd seen of them."

"Then what?" Kinth says, stroking his beard.

"*Then*, I went back to the city and paid a visit to the mansion."

"Pearl?"

"She was okay at first. A little shaken up, but okay," Miles replies.

"At first? What do you mean *at first*?"

Miles rubs his face in a concerned fashion. "I went there with the hopes of getting her outta there. Your brother is one card short of a full stack, but you know this. She wouldn't leave. I ended up getting caught, and then I received this little gift." He points to his bandaged arm.

"What happened to you?" Enrico asks.

Kinth scans the faces at the table.

"What do you think happened? They shot me!"

"Who shot you? My brother?" Kinth chimes in.

"Ha! No. You know as well as I do he would have an old lady do his dirty work before doing it himself. After I got shot, I fell out the window where I had been visiting Pearl. Luckily, I had my people with me, and so we went underground. They bandaged me up – yada, yada. Nothing I can't handle. I had plans to come back again to find you.

But then, I saw a group of your brother's goons taking someone . . . somewhere."

A hush falls over the table.

Looking down, Kinth begins to rub his face – pondering all that Miles has said.

Miles continues, "I was intrigued with all that was going on, so I followed the group quietly for a while. I wasn't close enough to see details, but I figured someone was about to get . . ." He takes one of his claws and motions it across his neck menacingly. "Then it hit me. That could have been Pearl or it could have been you. So, I continued to follow. I followed for as long as I could until I came across some wolves or something. I am in no condition to deal with that. I turned around, hoping to find help. Then, I stumbled onto this shit-hole and decided to rest a while."

One of the barkeep's helpers comes over and throws three baskets of bread onto the table. A moment later, he returns with a tray of ale and a handful of pitchers. "How you payin' for this, stranger?"

Reaching inside of his fur, Miles grabs a handful of shiny objects that looked like pieces of jewelry. He hands it to the helper. Inspecting the pieces, the helper nods and walks away.

"What did you give him?" Aldo asks.

"Just a little something I picked up along the way."

More quiet ensues as the fatigued prisoners replenish their energy with sugar and starch and ale. With each swallow, the group feels more rejuvenated.

"So . . . this island. What gives?" Miles says, breaking the silence after swallowing ale.

Kinth practically swallows his entire glass whole before placing it down and to his side. Clearing his throat, he inspects the room again before responding. "I don't know the path to that place, because I was unconscious most of the way. But my brother apparently had that place built. All types of people were in there. Seems like he put anyone in there who crossed or disobeyed him."

"Like these guys," Miles moves his claw erratically, pointing at the others at the table.

"Yeah. And . . . and father."

Practically falling off the bench, Miles spits out his ale across the table. He sprays Kinth and some others. "What?!"

"Shh. Shh. Don't cause any more of a scene, please. My father. He was alive."

"Well, shit! Where is he? Let's go! Oh my!"

"Miles, Miles, Miles," Kinth says emphatically, trying to calm him down.

"Mr. Miles, he WAS alive," Enrico says, emphasizing his statement by placing his hand in the middle of the table.

Looking at Kinth, Miles frowns. "What? What is he talking about, Kinth?"

"He's dead, Miles. He died not long after we reunited. It was as if . . . as if something wanted me to see him one last time before he took his final breath."

"So you're telling me that . . . all this time we thought your father was dead – he was rotting away in some shit-hole prison? And fuckin' Franklin put him there?!"

Kinth nods sorrowfully.

"I'll KILL HIM!"

"We need to bury him, Miles, before we do anything else."

"Where is he?"

"I put him somewhere safe, not too far from here. We need to head back soon, though, to get him and take him to my uncle's."

"Well, hurry up then! Let's go!"

Chapter 14

SAMMY, RAHZY & OTHERS – HOCK CITY

FROM HIS VANTAGE POINT INSIDE SADIE BELL'S, RAHZY watches as Sammy finishes his conversation with The Mantis. Both shake hands afterwards. Strutting back inside the venue, Sammy wears a smirk on his face.

"So? What did he say?" Rahzy inquires, walking behind him. "What did you agree to?"

Madam Pearl clears her throat aggressively, in an attempt to be included in the status report that Rahzy initiated.

"Cut that broad loose. We don't need her," Sammy says, beginning to gather up his things from the bar while taking another swig of ale. "Oh, and let them others go, too."

"Yes! Thank you!" One of the tied-up employees shouts excitedly.

"Sam!" Rahzy says, annoyed.

Turning around briskly, Sam says, "What?! What is it?!"

"What did he say?"

"Yeah. What *did* he say?" Madam Pearl chimes in from where she sits, still bound to a chair.

Hopping up onto the bar to sit, Sam drinks some more. He swishes around the powerful ale in his mouth. "So, apparently that insect-looking thing is the right-hand-man to this Guardian fellow."

"I basically told you that!" Pearl says with attitude.

"Shut up, already!" Sam yelps. He begins to whisper the rest of his words. "We don't need her or this Guardian person."

"Why not?"

"This Guardian guy was sending away any person he suspected of being human to some island."

"An island?" Rahzy says, perplexed.

"Yeah. There is a prison on this island full of humans! We go there, get them, and take them back to base. We will be treated like kings!"

"I see. How do you know this place is real? How do you know that humans are actually there? Do you trust him?"

Reaching into his pocket, Sam pulls out another tracking device which is similar to the one he put on the young Sadie Bell employee. "If he's lying, he's dying."

Rahzy chuckles. "But shouldn't we take her, just in case?"

"No, we can't. The deal was we free her, and he give us the intel. Besides, he agreed to wear one of these. When we get to this island and confirm the humans are there, I will deactivate it."

"How far away is this island?"

"Dunno. It will probably take a while. But if he leads us on a wild goose chase . . . kaboom!" Sam shouts, startling the Sadie Bell employees. Hopping down from the bar, Sam grabs his gear. "So let's go. Cut these people loose and let's get outta here."

One by one, Rahzy makes his rounds. He frees each of the Sadie Bell's employees first. At the window, Sam watches as The Mantis patiently awaits for Madam Pearl to be set free.

"Just like that? That's it?" Pearl says, rubbing her wrists.

Replying without turning toward her, Sam says, "Yeah. Get outta here. You been a pain in my ass. Good riddance."

Sadie Bell's employees run in various directions: some out the back of the venue; the rest through the front and down alley ways. Pearl walks quietly to the entrance. Following behind her, Rahzy disarms his weapons and holsters them. Sam gathers up his remaining items, filling up an empty jug with ale and pouring peanuts into a bag.

"Well hot damn! It took you long enough," Pearl steps down onto the street where The Mantis and his security stood. "What did you tell them?"

Mantis ignores Pearl, speaking over her shoulder to Sam who had made his way around Rahzy. "Is there anything else I can help you with, gentlemen? I take it that our deal will suffice?"

"Yeah, we are good," Sam holds up his hand and jiggles the tracking device.

"Well then. Please exit our fine city that way, and may the universe provide you with all that you are searching for. Peace and light." Mantis says curtly, before turning his attention to Pearl. "This way, Madam."

As Madam Pearl becomes surrounded by security, the Mantis watches as Sam and Rahzy are escorted through the main gate of the city. Mantis rejoins Pearl at the center of the security a few moments later.

"You wanna tell me what you told them? Better yet, tell me what the hell is goin' on?" Pearl huffs.

The Mantis takes a long pause before responding, sighing deeply. "Pearl, I'm leaving."

Stopping, Pearl puts her hands on her hips. "What? What you mean you're leaving?"

"At this moment, you are the overseer of the city. I . . . I have had enough of this place. It's time for me to move onto the next phase of my life."

"What is going on? You can't just leave without telling me somethin'."

"Most of what needs to be said needs to come from Franklin. Only your brother can tell you what you need to hear. But what I can provide you with . . .," Mantis says, putting one hand on Pearl's shoulder, ". . . is an apology –

for my part in why this place has become what it has. I have been far too loyal to your brother, for too long."

Scratching her brow, Pearl takes a step closer, "I . . . I don't understand."

"Everyone! Stop! Listen here, please!" Mantis directs his security. "From this moment forward, each of you – every unit, every role, and every position – report to Madam Pearl. The Guardian is not here and I am not sure when he will be returning. Pearl is his next of kin. She is fit to lead you. All decisions must go through her from this point. I will be leaving to tend to other affairs. Do you understand?"

A variance of confirmations are shouted by the guards in response.

Pearl has become dumbfounded. She stands with her mouth partially open. "Just tell me one thing. Is my father alive?"

Tightening his face in shame, The Mantis says, "He was the last time I saw him."

"Where will you go?"

"I am unsure. But don't plan to see me again. It's best for us both. I will take you to the mansion and gather my things. I need to move along before anything more happens here."

Nodding, Madam Pearl turns to look toward the gate of the city, watching as the gates close behind the two bounty hunters who had held her hostage for some time. She wonders what was next for them, and more importantly, for her.

Back at Guardian's Grove, Madam Pearl follows behind The Mantis through the main entrance. Security has positioned themselves at various points around the dwelling and have reconvened their normal procedures. Inside the Guardian's mansion, The Mantis has left Pearl alone. Meanwhile, he ventures into areas of the mansion only he and The Guardian would frequent, amongst other people on The Guardian's staff.

Pearl has made her way into the kitchen, wandering around somewhat aimlessly. She looks for a glass to pour herself something to drink, talking aloud to no one in particular. "I spent most of my adult life trying to avoid coming to this place. Never felt as if I fit in. Wasn't *smart enough to be with the boys*. So they thought. But apparently, staying away has left me clueless on what has been going on here." She sucks her teeth, shaking her head.

After finding a glass, she then quickly realizes that there was plenty of wine and ale in the cellar.

Once in the cellar, Pearl slowly walks down one of the long rows of untouched barrels of wine and ale. One row in particular wasn't damaged from all of the activity that occurred previously. She lets her fingers glide across the barrels as she looked at each one. At the end of each row are racks of bottled wines, ales and other mixture of drinks. Pearl grabs one of the bottles. Then, she heads back to the table toward the front of the room.

While sitting at the table, she reviews more of the documents that were scattered along the floor. She reaches inside her clothing, pulling out papers that she had originally gathered from this location. But then, it quickly dawned on her that she had left them with her uncle.

"Shit!" she aggressively whispers.

"What's wrong, Pearl?" Mantis says, entering the cellar, almost unnoticed.

"Damnit! You can't be sneaking up on me like that right now. My nerves are already shot!"

"I apologize. I just wanted to let you know that I am leaving. One last . . . goodbye, I guess."

"You really gon' leave?" Pearl stands. "Without telling me anything?"

The Mantis lowers his head.

"What about . . . what about that human? Why is he so important? Hmm? Why all this madness over him?"

"The human represents a change that your brother doesn't want. A change that . . . that threatens his control. His leadership. His ownership. Do you understand?"

Pearl plops back down in her seat. "Hmph. Whatever you say. I still don't get it. But I will figure it out."

"Well then, Pearl. I know we aren't fond of each other, but I do hope that the universe is kind to you. Please take this place and . . . do something with it. Improve it." The Mantis paces a bit, getting one last look at the cellar before he walks toward the steps leading to the upstairs floor.

"Tell me about *Uhmandra*," Pearl says randomly.

Stopping, The Mantis stands with his back turned for a moment before responding. "Uhmandra? I'm not —"

"Don't bullshit me, Mantis. You can't work for my brother for as long as you have and not know something."

"Pearl," Mantis sighs, turning around. "Some questions have dangerous answers. I truly don't know much about this. Nor does your brother. And that may be part of why things have happened the way they did."

"I found some papers down here the last time I was here. They looked like some sort of plans to build something. I don't know. Do they have something to do with that human?"

"Where are these papers now?"

"I . . . I lost them in the fields," Pearl stammers, unsure on whether to be upfront about the papers or not. Her trust for everyone around her has dwindled, even by her standards.

Looking visibly troubled by the news, Mantis walks towards Pearl. He stops at a small desk nearby. Reaching for a broken bottle of ale, he grabs the sharpest piece of glass from it. Placing his arm on the desk, he slams the sharp piece of glass into it with one swift motion. He gradually severs a portion of his arm from the rest of his body. Then, he then lifts up his wounded arm, allowing the tracking device to slide off.

"Oh shit! Why . . . why did you that?!" Pearl says, fearfully. She almost falls out of her chair.

"Don't worry. It will grow back, eventually," the Mantis says, as he wraps up the stump. He then reconvenes his stroll to the door. "Pearl . . . if nothing more, the most I can tell you is to be careful. I must be on my way. As of this moment, I don't exist in any capacity to this place. Take care of yourself."

Shocked by the display, Pearl watches Mantis walk away.

Chapter 15

MATHIAS - FETELA

MATHIAS PACES THE BOARDWALK INSIDE OF FETELA, watching the activity of his people just as much as he eyes the sky. The changes of it has provided a warming overcast but has troubled those within the city who have taken notice. Gazing at the surrounding hills and the mountains, mentally Mathias prepares himself for what's to come.

Bouncing around various scenarios, he wonders what could happen. Perhaps an ambush by the woman whom he did business with on many occasions, but knew little about?

Or other more violent troubles by any number of unknown threats in the flatlands?

Pausing, he snaps his fingers after having a proverbial light bulb moment. "I'm not waiting on her," he thinks aloud. Storming back in the direction of the drop tower, he mentally catalogs his plan. As he looks up, he notices his beautiful bedmates looking down at him from above. He waves at them, smiling subtly. *A quickie would be nice*, he thinks.

Before he can get to the base of the tower, a handful of his team of security shouts to get his attention. "Mathias! We have some news - an update!"

"Yes? What is it?" Mathias asks inquisitively.

"We were able to track the woman . . . the one with, uh, no name."

Mathias continues to walk away. "Good! When did you'll do this?"

"Some of our travelers who were already out have returned. They informed us of the route after we shared our concerns."

"Excellent! Let's follow her. I'm heading up to get my things now."

"Following her on the same trail would be unwise," One of the guards, a hulking woman, jogs to catch up with the group.

"What do you recommend, then?" Mathias replies, folding his arms.

Another woman with a smaller, athletic physique from the group chimes in on the update. "We found another route. It should possibly take us to her location, without us being seen. It is around those mountains, over the hills of Malandis." The woman points.

"But the fastest route is a straight line, which would be the line directly behind her." Mathias asserts. "We just need to be prepared."

"Yes, but we risk an attack going in the same direction. They could have set traps."

Mathias sighs. "Okay. Saddle the beetles. Arm yourselves as discreetly as you can. We ride shortly."

An elder, who had been silent up until this point, approaches. "Won't riding the beetles bring unwanted attention?"

Others who had also been silent groan in agreement.

Speaking emphatically, Mathias says, "I understand that the beetles are not the best choice. But if we must go around the mountain, we must go around quickly. I can't afford to give this woman any time to prepare. We will be ready . . . for whatever we encounter."

The group hesitantly nods, dispersing in various directions.

Several yards away, a grimy, hole-ridden circus tent stands inside of a separate, guarded fence. Inside, some of Mathias's other team members train and feed several massive desert beetles. The beetles are about the size of elephants. All are identically shaped with the same core anatomy: six legs – a round, wide body, horns and large wings.

Some of the beetles are resting, while being chained to posts. Others pace the open area. A tall man, about half the height of the beetles, feed them various things from a bucket. Mostly the beetles are fed smaller insects and rodents they eat by the handful.

Noticing the group of security approaching, the man puts down the bucket and walks over to a row of bars installed against the tent. Several large saddles are draped across the bars and along with muzzles. They're next to leather roping tools and additional tools needed to control the large insects for travel.

"Something told me that these guys would be needed soon, especially after that woman visited again," the beetle wrangler says.

The husky woman from before steps inside the gated area. Walking up to one of the beetles, she rubs it aggressively to cause its wings to flap. "Did you see something?"

"No, no. But I feel something, because the animals feel something."

Curiously, the group glances at each other.

"We need to travel quickly. Mathias believes the beetles will get us to our destination faster."

"Yes, yes. They will." The wrangler turns around slowly, running the rope through the saddles. "But keep in mind that these beetles aren't used to the wild. If they are spooked in any way, they will fly off. They may even attack you, should they feel you are leading them into danger."

"Oh, I think we will be alright," the woman chuckles, flexing her large arm.

"It will take more than just strength!"

"Just saddle 'em up so we can go!"

The beetle wrangler continues to rope the saddles, tying them down atop the back of the beetles. He wraps the rope around the legs and backs. After completing each one, he whispers something quietly to the beetle.

Moments later, Mathias surprises the group. He has gathered his travel gear faster than expected. "Are we ready?"

"Almost. The handler here is having a hard time letting them go."

Mathias walks towards one of the beetles, patting the wrangler on the shoulder as he moves by. "As he should. One who cares for his work also cares for how others care for it as well."

The wrangler saddles up the last beetle and backs away. "Please return them in one piece. It took some time to mend the wing on that one the last time you went out," he says.

"Understood," Mathias nods as he climbs up the side of the beetle. After strapping in his gear and his feet onto each side of the saddle, he snaps the rein. "Ya! Let's go!"

"Please feed them regularly!" The wrangler tries to get one last instruction out before his statement falls onto the ears of the wind. He finishes his statement to himself, "You don't want to end up their meal."

One by one, the beetles exit the large tent accompanied by their rider. They travel down one of the pathways and through Fetela's main gate. These large creatures are a challenge to control, but Mathias and his group of skilled rangers, trackers and mercenaries do their best. Mathias has the most experience, having ridden one previously.

Traveling for some time, up and over various hills, the beetles seem to slow down on their own. The slow pace makes for a quiet moment to talk.

"Mathias, I believe they need to eat," one of the unit members assert.

"Okay. A little further," Snapping the reins again, Mathias causes his beetle to speed up a little, but not by much. "We can give them a rest up there."

"What is our plan once we find where the woman is located? I'm sure that she isn't alone, despite how she seems to travel to us."

Mathias doesn't respond at first. Instead, he visibly processes the sentiments of his team member. "We watch. Take notes of the place. I may have to go in alone."

"You think that's a good idea?"

"Can't risk all of us being trapped in the middle of a fight. Worst case scenario, someone will need to hang back to make contact with Fetela."

Mathias's beetle slows to almost stopping, strolling casually. In front of the group, just over the sandy hills around the Malandis Mountain, is the faint flicker of light. There's what appears to be smoke rising into the air. The smell of food gradually crosses Mathias's nose the closer he and the others close in on the location.

As the group gets closer, they descend a hill. Various bodies can be seen moving about on a sandy road, near a cluster of buildings. Various objects can be seen, piercing from the sand as the group continues to walk the beetles closer.

Rubbing her arm, the husky woman's skin begins to tingle. The hair on her forearm slowly stands at attention. "Mathias! We need to find somewhere to tie the beetles, away from any activity down there. Something tells me we may be in mixed company."

"Yes. I agree. But where we tie them can't be far," Mathias replies, examining the area. "We need to be able to saddle again quickly."

Gazing some yards away, a member from the group notices another small mountain with various nooks and arid foliage around it. "Mathias, look. Over there. That should be a good place."

Without saying a word, Mathias snaps his reins, causing his beetle to flap its wings for the first time during the journey. The beetle hovers low to the ground, but briskly in the direction of the mountain. Jumping down, Mathias dismounts the beetle and ties it to multiple trees.

"How will we ensure they will stay here? These ropes are a mere illusion in comparison to their size," someone says.

Pulling out a mechanical bow and multiple arrows, another from Mathias's unit aims toward the side of the mountain. Releasing the arrow, he strikes three large mountain goats that had been traveling as a group. They had been grazing and watching from the distance. The goats shriek almost in unison, just before they begin to tumble over one another. Then, they fall to the base of the mountain nearby. The soldier walks over to the location, grabbing two of the goats and holding them up by their hind legs. "These should keep them occupied for a bit."

Tossing them in the middle of the beetles, the large creatures unhurriedly approach and begin eating slowly.

Mathias chuckles, "Yes, but not long."

Mathias leads the group some yards away, cautiously back toward the vicinity of the sand-covered roads and buildings. Noticing much activity was at one of the venues, he says nothing. Instead, he only nods in the direction of the building. Acknowledging the silent order, the rest fall in behind him.

Pushing through the wooden door opening, Mathias walks in gently and stands right aside the entrance. Observing the room, he notices that things appear to be peaceful. Patrons are enjoying quiet conversation and a beverage, while getting something to eat. Trying to keep a low profile, the last of his team walks in. They let the wooden doors slam behind them. A sudden quiet falls over the room, with all eyes on the tall man who has a bunch of people with him.

"Don't mind us. We're just looking for a tasty beverage!" Mathias says.

The quiet roar of conversations reconvene as Mathias' group casually strolls down the aisle between several tables. They pass by one that consisted of an old man, a kid and someone else to whom they didn't really pay any attention. One of the waitresses stands near as well, in what seems to be a growing argument or discussion. Mathias raises a brow at the sight, but keeps walking.

Sitting down at one of the semi-crowded tables, Mathias and his team are quiet as they examine the room. One of his husky lieutenants pulls out a small book and opens it. Upon opening it, the inked wording appears gradually anytime enough light shines upon it. The man pulls one of the lanterns nearby closer, causing a hand drawn map to fully appear.

Smiling, the lieutenant leans in closer to Mathias, "We aren't too far from our route. We should be okay."

"Good. Get a beverage and keep your ears open for anything that might help us," Mathias says.

Chapter 16

KINTH, MILES & OTHERS – NORTH OF HOCK CITY

HOW THEY MANAGED TO WALK INTO THE PUB AND LEAVE without a fight amazed Kinth, causing him to wonder more about it. The obvious reason was because of Miles. Miles simply had a way with words; a certain charisma that many found oddly attractive and respected.

At this point, Kinth and Miles, along with Aldo and Enrico, lead the group of prison escapees toward the northern area near Hock City. All the while, they used the dim light of the menacing sky as a guide.

Before their travels in this direction and after spending more time within the drunken environment, Kinth had discussed the details with Miles about his father over the taste of bread and ale. Kinth has managed to return to his father's body. He removed him without waking a soul in the small town and without any further confrontations.

The local woman wasn't around, as wasn't anyone else – which was something else that Kinth found unusual. Only the chatter of critters and wild animals moving about the corners and hills. Nonetheless, he and the group have closed in on his uncle's neighborhood, the same area where his father once lived many, many cycles ago.

The two had been neighbors when Kinth was much younger. Only a few streets separated their homes. Most of the buildings, including his childhood home, had been all or partly demolished, except for his uncle's.

Approaching his uncle's home, Kinth felt strange. It was as if he could feel the presence of something or someone else. Slowing his pace to crawl, he inspects the area which causes the others to take notice.

"What is it?" Aldo asks.

Slow to respond, Kinth replies, "Nothing." He begins to walk again but abruptly stops once more. He stops right at the beginning of the walkway that leads to his uncle's home.

Miles looks over his shoulder attentively.

"What is it?" Aldo asks again.

"I gotta say, you got me a bit concerned, too," Miles chimes in, moving a little faster than before. "I really wish we came this way underground."

Enrico makes his way to the front. "Why did we stop again? Is everything okay?"

The wind begins to stir, causing the foliage to move. Debris moves across the ground and through the air quickly. Crows watch and caw, sitting nearby on the remains of a light pole. Familiar moments that Kinth had seen plenty of times before, causing him to ball his fists. He tightens his hands enough that the redness of his knuckles glow slightly.

Aldo watches in a slight panic, "Kinth! What is it, man?!"

"No cause for alarm!" A woman's voice shouts quietly from some ways away. The color of the sky gradually changes again over the flatlands.

"Who speaks?!" Kinth replies, unable to see the surroundings clearly.

"Oh boy," Miles moves behind Kinth slowly.

Other escapees prepare themselves as they listen to Kinth speak to the open area as if he was conversing with something hidden. Various parts of the neighborhood begin to glow as small amber-colored circles appear within the brush and on the sides of buildings.

The woman's voice becomes louder but, in the language, with which Kinth was more familiar. After realizing that it was the Desert Dwellers, he responds using the same tongue while remaining alert.

Kira then reveals herself from behind a wall created by her fellow Ekladi people. They had been standing together, holding hands, and stirring the wind to create a protective camouflage around the group.

Taking a step back, Kinth squints to see the woman behind the voice as she approaches. Other members of her group approach as well from various locations around the neighborhood.

"Who are you? I've never seen you amongst these Dwellers before," Kinth asks.

Exhaling deeply, Kira replies after inspecting the home to which the group was near, "Yes, I normally stay clear of these lands unless it's absolutely necessary. But you have clearly met my people before."

"Yes, and it wasn't a pleasant meeting. What do you want?" Kinth raises his head assertively.

Stepping closer, Kira says, "If you are looking for your human friend, you won't find him here."

Several of the escapees begin to whisper with deep feelings of amazement and confusion. Many of them had been locked away for some time. Most had only heard second and third-hand stories about the legendary humans. Still, they had never came close to anyone who had seen one, let alone seen one themselves. And yet, more mention of them.

"What is she talkin' 'bout, Kinth?" Aldo steps to Kinth's side.

Exhaling deeply, Kinth takes a moment to collect his thoughts. "Enrico, take everyone inside that home. We will finish what we came here to do in a bit." He glances over at his father's body, laying peacefully in tall brush nearby.

Kira notices the body as well. "Seems you loss someone during your journey. I'm sorry."

"A great loss," Kinth replies serenely, nodding.

Miles interjects aggressively. "Enough small talk, toots. We have traveled a long way. Honestly, I'm ready to sit down. You and your sand folk seem to have something to say, so say it."

After the remaining escapee enters the home, Kinth approaches Kira to speak to her closely. "Where is the human and the boy?"

"Yeah, and – and what's your name?" Aldo stammers, chiming in as if he knows what's going on.

"My name is Kira. These people represent my Ekladi family. But you more commonly know us as Desert Dwellers, sand people and probably other negative connotations."

Miles gasps, stepping backwards.

"Please, no need to worry yourself," Kira says, just before she climbs a large stone upon which was flat enough to sit. She crosses her legs and relaxes. Others in her group do the same nearby as well, as they stand around her to keep watch. "I was just telling your friends during our journey that you have met my people before. And how you have learned some of our way of speaking. You are from that station, correct? The one off of Highway 99?"

Slowly kneeling, Kinth sticks one of his hands in the sand and soil. He grabs a small amount of it before rubbing both hands together, sitting before he responds. "Yep. That would be me."

"Alright. This is odd. Can we fast-forward through all this small talk, please?" Miles paces nervously.

Glancing to his side, Kinth says, "I agree with my friend here."

"The human and the boy were moving across these lands erratically. They were in danger. My people recognized them from several cycles ago. We believe they left this location when we crossed paths. We offered to help them."

"Help them how?"

"To help the human get home," Kira replies.

Kinth diverts his attention to Miles. "Does this sound right to you?"

"I guess," Miles shrugs. "After we left you in that cellar, I brought Jesse and the human here so they could speak to the old man. I didn't come with them inside."

Leaning forward, Kira leans and rests her arms on her legs. "What is this cellar that you speak of? Are you from inside the city, Miles?"

"Unfortunately."

Kira scans over the faces of the group before continuing. "We lead them to the Biyo Bridge."

"Got it," Kinth says, standing to his feet and visibly tired of talking. He begins to walk away.

"There is more."

Groaning, Kinth stops in his tracks. "Like?"

"The Guardian is following them," Kira says distinctly.

"What?!" Miles huffs. "How? How did he –"

"I told him where they were."

"What?!" Miles shouts again. "Do you realize what you have done?!"

Kinth steps toward Kira aggressively, "Why would you do that? Do you know how much we have all been through just to get that kid to safety?"

Various members of the Ekladi people quickly come to Kira's side, prepping themselves for a potential tussle.

Holding her hands out to her side, Kira pauses before responding. "It's okay. It's okay. Please. Everyone just relax." She stands before continuing. "There is an older man with your human. The Guardian seems to have been just as interested in this man, as he was the human. I told him where the human was, but not where the human was going. Unless your friend stops for too long, he should be well ahead and close to home."

"Older man?" Miles looks at Kinth briefly before pulling him aside. "Kinth, your uncle isn't here. Do you really think he is with them? If your brother is out here somewhere, he might have someone watching this place right now."

Pondering all the information, Kinth turns his attention back toward Kira. He quickly studies her demeanor and reflects on the various encounters he had with the Desert Dwellers previously. Somehow, he is still alive when Kira and her people could have tried to eliminate him many, many cycles ago.

"Why did you come here to tell me this?" Kinth asks.

"To proposition you."

"Proposition?" Miles folds his arms.

Clasping her hands together, Kira continues, "Help us enter the city, and we will help you."

"How do you know that we need any help? Seems like you need more help than we do if you came here."

Sighing, Kira drops her head bitterly. "My mother is a slave to The Guardian, just like some of the family of my people."

"Everyone in that city is a slave in some regard," Kinth snaps back.

"Hey, hey, hey. C'mon," Miles chimes in shamefully. "Sheesh. It's bad but not all of us enjoy it."

"My mother and some others are being held against their will, working for The Guardian. We must rescue them."

Stroking his beard, Kinth says, "And because The Guardian is away – out here somewhere – you feel it's the perfect time."

"Yes."

"We've come too far in this direction to go back that way right now, especially after finding this out. At this point, we need to get to my uncle and the others before The Guardian. If you're willing to assist us in doing that, we will help you retrieve your people from inside those walls."

"Ah geez," Miles shakes his head.

"Could you possibly tell us of a way we could get into the city discreetly? Then we can all go our separate ways," another from the Ekladi group replies. "Our abilities work well out here in the open, but within those walls we are unsure."

"Assuming The Guardian has put his security on high alert, just approaching the walls would be a death sentence.

Or, at the very least a fight." Kinth continues to stroke his chin, pacing some. Stopping, he stares at Miles.

"Oh you gotta be kidding me!" Miles slaps his sides frustratingly.

"It's the only way they can get in the city. The same way the kid brought the human inside."

"Which way was this?" Kira interjects.

Walking in small circles, Miles replies, "The tunnels. But I'm not going through those. I like our own. The ones we created. Those other ones have become a mess ever since your brother put those gatekeepers in them. Creeps me out. Plus you need special keys and stuff. I can take you, but my way."

Kira looks at her trusted advisors for approval, who nod in return. "If that is our only, quickest option, then we will take it."

Also nodding, Kinth pats Miles on the shoulder. "I'm not sure what's waitin' on us out there. You know your way around the city better. So, lead them. I will see you when we return."

Miles scratches his head. "Yeah. I told the misses I was done after I helped the human. Sheesh! I need a break."

Turning his attention back to Kira, Kinth speaks insistently. "One more condition."

"And that would be?"

Calming his tone, Kinth continues, "Let us borrow a couple of your people since they know which way the human went. We will need more muscle than you will if The Guardian is truly away from the city."

Glancing over her shoulder, Kira looks to one of her people for agreement. Without any words or physical acknowledgement, she replies, "We can work that out. Just stay your course. My people will find you."

Nodding, Kinth begins to back away. "I have something I need to do first."

"Yeah. Give us a moment, sweetheart. If you and yours could wait for me down there a bit, I will call your number shortly," Miles chimes in, pointing in the direction closer toward Hock City.

Unamused, Kira nods. She steps toward Kinth before he could get too far away, and extends her hand. "Till we meet again." The two shake hands just before she walks gently away in the direction as instructed, members of her group around her.

"I don't have a good feeling about this," Miles whispers, after double-checking that there was some distance between him and Kinth, and the Ekladi people.

"Honestly, I haven't had a good feeling touch my skin in many cycles. I damn near rotted away in that station. And again at that damn island. It wasn't until I saw my father again and had closure that I felt . . . peace. And you know what it took for me to see him again?"

"What?" Miles scratches his face, listening attentively.

Pacing again and visibly gathering his thoughts, Kinth replies, "That human."

"Yeah, yeah. I get it. It takes a crisis . . ."

"Exactly. I know you have been asked to do a lot right now. But hopefully this is it. Finished. So let's do what we need to and get outta here."

"I second that," Aldo says, listening observantly.

Chapter 17

THE GUARDIAN & TEAM - FLATLANDS

MAKING THEIR WAY ACROSS THE DESERT FLATLANDS, THE Guardian sluggishly follows behind his team, ascending and descending various peaks and stone-filled valleys, after the group had made minor changes to their route. One of his guards confessed to hearing some others in the bar talking before they left. They had spoken about another remote location – a hostel that had food. But more importantly, it had beds for them to recharge.

While this hostel wasn't too far, it was in a slightly different direction than The Guardian had intended to travel. Because of his slightly drunken state and because of the shot of ale the bartender had supplied him, The

Guardian had agreed to make this destination their next stopping point.

During their travels, The Guardian's mind began running wild, filling itself with various, random thoughts of the present and past. It was as if the ale he drank was also a serum or hallucinogen that took some time to activate. His thoughts spewed out of control after he noticed a tree which appeared quite familiar to him. In fact, he hadn't seen it since his time in the city. Various foliage and shrubbery was scarce in the city, except for around his mansion. So, seeing this particular tree did something to him.

The tree, being a large mesquite, was very similar to what he had seen during his childhood. Long before the event, he and his siblings would run around their backyard. They would swing from an old tire that The Guardian's father had tied to one of this tree's limbs. One of the last trees like this stood the days and weeks following the event. His father held onto it for as long as he could before it seemed to have deteriorated on its own, despite his care for it doing yardwork.

As his mind flashed again, The Guardian cursed under his breath. At this moment, he thought of the various punishments he endured for his behavior during his teenage and young adult years. How he accused his father of favoritism any chance he could get. The several times he went missing for days because of his anger and the numerous therapy sessions.

Another flash.

This time, he has visions of the nights following the event where the object pierced the sky. He remembered watching his father stand on their front porch, where he would stare at their neighbors who were in distress. He recalled his father's confusion on their change in behavior; worrisome and confused. The fleeing of those who thought they could run away from the terror. The erratic movements of people scrambling to throw as many of their belongings into cars and drive until their rear lights faded into the distance.

Shaking his head, The Guardian attempted to snap out of his cycle of thoughts. He said something under his breath again; inaudible.

Then he vaguely remembered being very small. Sitting in a chair next to a man and a woman, another man sat across the room and another woman behind a desk. The conversation, although inaudible and muffled in his mind, is vivid as he remembers the environment.

"No, no, no. Please!" he shouts to himself in distress.

"Sir – you okay?" a member of his unit asks.

Waving off the question, The Guardian snaps back to reality. But then, he quickly falls back into his thoughts. This time, he reflects on his mother. After the event, her behavior also changed. At first, she was tired and sluggish. She didn't do what she normally did around the house: making meals, cleaning, and complaining aloud about a character in the romance novels she loved to read. She almost suddenly became angry – so disturbed, in fact, that The Guardian's father would have to keep her locked in her room until he was able to calm her.

More abstract reflections occur.

Another team member interjects, "This place shouldn't be much farther."

On an adjacent path several miles away, the Cepha man – who had previously lounged at the remote bar - has moved briskly across the lands. He's reached his base at the Ifera Medical Park. Unknowingly, The Guardian had been talking to this Cepha man at the bar, unaware that he was one of Hakra's many scouts.

His duties as a scout included luring subjects into various traps and returning them to Hakra. It was quite similar to Feeza and her trades with Mathias. Noticing the odd visit from The Guardian at the bar and overhearing his conversation, the Cepha man left in a scurry. Quickly he used his abilities to traverse the hills toward Ifera.

Arriving not long after Feeza, the Cepha man made his way to Hakra's quarters. Noticing the secretary leisurely moving about the office, the Cepha man aggressively questions her. "Where is he? Is he in?" he asks without waiting for a response. He then pushes through the office doors.

"Go. Go right in," the secretary says without a care.

Noticing the empty office, the Cepha man returns to the lobby once more. "Where is he?"

"He took Feeza and the others to the lab," the secretary replies dryly.

The Cepha man doesn't say a word at first. Instead, he studies the secretary's demeanor. While doing so, he seems to listen to the subtle sounds of the room and the building. Briskly leaving the office, he heads toward the elevator that has access to the lab. "Since when does he take her to the lab?!"

Moving around the lab casually, Hakra continues his intense questioning of Feeza. "Your trader friend is curious; so curious, in fact, that he would like to come to this place?

Hmm. Well, I guess he is making your job easier. Especially if he has no more subjects as you assume."

"What do you recommend I do? What do I tell him?"

Hakra paces the pathway, looking over the various technicians' shoulders who are dressed in various lab attire. Their clothes are made from leftover uniforms that were left behind many cycles before. Undeniably, they are scraps of clothing, tubing and ventilation devices that were gathered over some time.

Whispering something in one of the technician's ears, Hakra stops and turns his attention back toward Feeza. Visibly he is prepared to respond, but he is interrupted by the sound of the lab's doors opening and of heavy footsteps drawing near.

"Hakra! We have a problem!" the Cepha man shouts before the doors close behind him.

"Wonderful! More great news," Hakra replies, brazenly. "Let me guess. One of our suppliers has been asking questions about our business here?"

Feeza turns to face the Cepha man as he approaches. But then, she turns back to Hakra. "You gave him access to the lab, and not me?!"

"Quiet," Hakra snaps.

The Cepha man rushes to the area. "Yes. But I have other, different news."

"Wait a minute. Have you been following me?" Feeza abruptly asks. "Hakra, you had him follow me?"

Pausing what he initially wanted to say, the Cepha man replies to Feeza first. "It was only a precaution, just in case you needed any assistance. And I did not follow you on your most recent trip. I'm surprised to see you back so soon."

"But how did you know about what has happened? About my dealings in Fetela?"

"*Our* . . . dealings," Hakra says smugly, sitting on the edge of one of the lab tables. "Seems that during your trips you have forgotten your place.

A bit deflated, Feeza drops her head.

"I have been blending in with other traders at Fetela. I go there sometimes regardless of your mission. I have my own orders. I overheard Mathias's people talking about you. You have quite the reputation there, but that is not why I am here," the Cepha man replies.

Hakra adjusts his posture. Based on his body language, he is visibly frustrated. "So . . . why are you here? Please share your news."

"I apologize for my visit without notice, but there is an armed group searching for some missing people. They are searching for people from Hock City and Longleaf and are not far from here. I worry they may discover our base."

"You worry? Why?" Hakra rises from the table, walking over to the man. He places both hands on the man's shoulders. "Do you not have faith in my leadership?"

"No, sir. Never. I would never doubt you or your work here," the Cepha man replies innocently. He trembles for a moment before collecting himself. "It's just . . . this is no ordinary armed group."

"Oh no? How so?" Hakra steps back.

Leaning into whisper, the Cepha man says something inaudible to everyone else in the room.

"Is that right?'" Hakra replies smugly. "No worries. Just inform our security. Tell them to keep a special eye for anything strange."

Nodding, the man quickly leaves the lab. Feeza watches him closely as he leaves, lowering her eyes to gather her thoughts. Before she could come up with anything, the old woman takes a few steps toward the center of the lab's testing area.

HAKRA

"So . . . how are the tests coming along?" the old woman asks, attempting to eliminate some of the tension in the room. "Any progress since we've seen you last?"

Hakra begins to pace the testing area, moving around his technicians who have been keeping a close eye on various machinery filled with various buttons, levers, and lights. Various subjects are unconscious inside of individual cylinders, connected to one even larger cylinder in the center of the platform. Various fluid runs in and out of these subjects through small wires and tubing. Certain fluid runs into a rectangular machine while other fluid is routed through the cylinder upward.

"We have made progress with our genetic extraction testing. I believe that, with a few more subjects, our testing can achieve what I would like it to," Hakra looks at Feeza intensely. "But I guess more patience is required. Until our guests arrive. "

Chapter 18

LANGSTON, JESSE & WINSTON - HOSTEL

IT WAS AS IF SOMEONE HAD POURED CONCRETE AROUND Langston's desire to speak, and threw it into the deepest end of a pool. His stomach sunk and his skin grew flush, as he listened to the woman affectionately say his name more than once. All were words that seemed like a foreign language.

"Langston? Langston, is it really you?" Small, glowing tears roll down the woman's cheeks.

HAKRA

The beautiful, familiar voice — the sweetest sound Langston had heard in some time - surprised and distracted him. It was so distracting, in fact, that he didn't notice the group of people entering the front entrance of the remote bar. But Winston did, and he glanced at them as they entered.

"Young Langston, you have a visitor. Langston!" Winston says, after slapping his hand on the table one time, hard enough to break Langston's gaze. He motions his head at the young woman who seemed to be just as star struck as Langston.

Moving his head sharply, Langston mouths something faint at first while standing to his feet. Without warning, he was then able to speak, as if someone had revived his voice. "Talicia?!" Grabbing her tightly, he embraces her cheek to cheek. The two hug as Langston spins her around briskly.

"Is it really you?" Talicia says once more, grabbing Langston's face with both her hands as her eyes moisten. "I never thought I would see you again!" Her excitement begins to be noticed by some nearby patrons, who had been gradually rubber-necking all the activity inside.

Langston stares at the young woman with tender eyes. He caresses her long, thick locks of hair which is twisted with small, intricate charms dangling from various strands. "I can't . . . I can't believe it's you! I didn't think I would see you again. It feels like . . . I haven't seen you –"

"I know! I know. We have been looking for you!"

The old man, upon noticing the attention from the other patrons, leans onto the table. "Langston, please be so kind to *sit*. Introduce us to your friend." He does something weird with his eyes, scans the room and nods his head.

Langston excitedly obliges. "Sorry, sorry. Talicia, this is Jesse and Mr. Winston. Some new friends that I have made recently."

"Hi," Talicia responds softly, sitting on the edge of the bench near Jesse.

Jesse admires her hair, touching it gently from behind. Her hair responds to his touch, moving slowly around his fingers. It causes him to pull his hand back rapidly.

"Well, I see you guys know each other," the waitress winks at Jesse as she returns. She pushes a wobbly, wheeled basket. Inside of the basket are various beverages held within wooden and steel cups, and bowls of soup. She also has thick loaves of bread and other snacks. She places everything on the table gradually. "Here is your food."

"Thank you kindly," replies the old man. "Oh this smells intriguing!"

Talicia struggles to look away from Langston, turning her head to her waitress friend. "Thanks, boo."

"You got it, girl. Let me know if y'all need anything else."

"I'm so glad that you are alive," Talicia turns back toward Langston. She leans into him, resting her face on his shoulder. "We have been searching for you for so long."

As the two talk, Jesse slides each cup, plate and set of utensils down to everyone at the table.

"Well aren't you the polite one," Talicia says excitedly, before turning back toward Langston. Softening her voice, she finishes her original statement. "I thought you might be gone forever. Or . . . "

"Don't say it. I know."

Grabbing his bowl and cup, the old man slides closer to the two. He motions to a stranger to switch places with him.

"But I was here first!" the random man shouts.

"Oh here! You big cry baby!" Winston replies, throwing the random man a large piece of his bread.

The man nods before moving, chewing the bread insistently.

"Do you remember anything before you went missing?" Talicia asks, after smirking at the old man's change of seating.

"I was hoping you could tell me," Langston replies, rubbing Talicia's hand gently. "My mind has like . . . gaps in it. I remember home, momma and of course you. But nothing right before."

Talicia sighs. "Just before you went missing, some of our friend's went missing, too." She leans down, grabbing a bag from the floor.

"Oh no! Really?" Langston says, worriedly. An awkward silence falls upon the table. "They never returned?"

Shaking her head slowly, Talicia places her bag on the table, resting both of her arms on it. She takes a moment to let Langston process things before taking out several pieces of paper.

"I had an artist friend of mine draw these up. I put a lot of these around Longleaf and in other places. That's why I'm here," Talicia says as she gently places the papers in front of Langston. The papers have Langston's likeness drawn on them, along with faces of their other missing friends. The word MISSING is bolded at the top, with additional wording at the bottom. "You and I and some others were looking for our friends. Then, you went missing. I almost gave up because I felt hopeless without you."

Langston begins to shake his head softly. He tries to make sense of the whirlwind of activities he has been through as well as this new information. Frustration grows inside him, so much so that his eyes begin to well up. "Man, what is going on?"

Touching Langston's hand softly, Talicia replies, "What do you remember?"

Langston explained the status of his journey, sharing the details of how he met Jesse and Winston, Kinth and Madam Pearl, Miles and The Guardian. The Desert Dwellers, Hock City and the struggles between.

Talicia's confusion could be seen on her face. "So . . . someone took you and you managed to get away?"

"I guess. Like I said, I couldn't remember much after I had woken up or after Jesse found me. Mr. Winston believes this has something to do with the hospital gown I was wearing. Maybe . . . maybe I escaped. I don't know."

Sighing deeply, the old man chimes in after taking another sip of his soup. "Young Langston, I believe we need to move this conversation to a more secluded area."

"Why?"

Clearing his throat, Winston says, "I just remembered that there is more to what I was telling you when we were making our way here. Ms. Talicia, could you please have your friend move us to another area?"

Talicia acknowledges the request but doesn't respond. Instead, she gets up from the table and walks through the crowded rows of people to where her waitress-friend was standing.

Back at the table, Langston moves closer to where the old man was sitting. "What's going on? What do you need to tell me?" he whispers.

Jesse sips from his cup, seemingly unbothered by the conversation, or anything else in the room for that matter.

Looking at Langston, the old man holds a finger over his mouth.

"Hey, you guys! C'mon! This way! We can sit over here," Talicia says, waving them over to an area in the corner. She runs back toward them to grab her belongings. After grabbing what she thought was all of the papers, she accidentally drops one sheet which was loose within her grasp. The paper floats gradually before falling at the feet of a man. As she walks behind Langston and the others, she doesn't notice the man sliding the paper closer to him on the floor, using his foot.

It was kind of hard to keep up with everything going on, with all the quiet but energetic laughter and conversations happening across the venue. Furthermore, more people were coming in and out the front entrance.

Once at the secluded corner table, the old man reconvenes, "Now, where were we? Ah, yes." He checks over his shoulder, noticing the man reading the dropped paper. "I met some locals on my way to the bridge where we reconnected."

"Okay. So?" Langston says, sitting back.

"One of them informed me that some of his people have gone missing as well. He believes that the activity is taking place somewhere near a strange mountain in Dyadika."

"I've heard of that place!" Talicia excitedly whispers. "But nobody believed it existed. It was like . . . like –"

"An urban legend," Langston interjects.

"What's an urban legend?" Jesse asks inquisitively.

Langston stares blankly at the table. "I don't know, really. I guess like a spooky story."

The old man chuckles. "A story, indeed! It can be spooky or fun but it may not be real! Or it could be so real, that people are scared to speak of its truth!"

No one else at the table laughs along with Winston. They are instead seemingly worried about many things.

"Buck up, children. Everything will be fine," Winston adds.

Trying to make sense of it all, Langston says, "Well, I'm glad we are all here, together."

"Indeed, my young friend!"

With a bit of pain in her eyes, Talicia looks at Langston fondly. Before she can chime in with her own thoughts to what Langston said, however, a tall and slender man approached with a piece of paper in his hands.

"Pardon my intrusion, but is this yours?" The man holds up the paper to display it to the table. Before anyone could respond, he continues. "May I sit, so that we can we talk?"

Chapter 19

KINTH, MILES & OTHERS – UNCLE'S HOUSE

THE SKY HAS FLUCTUATED BETWEEN VARIOUS SHADES OF darkness since Kinth and the others arrived. Everyone at the home in North Hock is either quiet or somber, mostly due to Kinth's final farewell acts to the man who once fathered him. The man also fathered many others, in a way, including strangers he met while being held captive at Delrusia Island.

In the open field where Kinth once lived as a child, in a home which no longer standing, he and some others dug a grave in the open field by the home. After placing his father in the grave, along with several moments of silence, soil was reapplied. It covered the body for its eternal rest. Kinth whispered something to himself as he took a knee, grabbing some of the remaining soil and gently throwing it over the grave.

Miles also shared a few words, speaking to the grave as if his old friend could hear him. Then, he spoke to Kinth privately. The two shared a couple of laughs, reminiscing over various moments in their long history of knowing each other – like the first time Kinth's father brought Miles home and introduced him to his then teenage and young adult children. His kids wore odd and stunned facial expressions like clothing for weeks, looking at the sight of a talking animal.

There is a break in their shared laughter, after Kinth remembers his mother. Flashes of her death flow through his mind. He doesn't say anything about her aloud, other than saying her name quietly to himself. Miles patted him on the arm to comfort him as best as he could. It was pretty tough to console such a large person from his position, but he did his best.

"You goin' to be alright?" Miles asks. "Sometimes even the toughest among us need to let it out."

Kinth looks down, exhaling heavily, "Yeah. I should be alright. There is more I need to tell you when we meet again. There's not enough time to share it now."

Miles begins to walk away. "Okay. Fair enough. We better get to it. Too much lingering out here is not good."

Nodding, Kinth moves toward the rear door of the home to reconnect with the others.

"Be safe, my friend. See you soon," Miles shouts, nearing Kira and the other Ekladi people who had been waiting.

Waving, Kinth enters the home. He watches from a window inside as Miles and the others leave. With growing suspicion and anger, Kinth notices that his uncle's home had been ransacked.

Aldo approaches. "Doesn't look good in here." He walks around the back room, moving pieces of broken furniture, books, and papers.

"What happened?" Enrico chimes in. He and some of the other prisoners have been resting at various places on the main floor.

Frowning, Kinth paces this area. He bounces around thoughts of what could have happened. It wasn't too hard to tell. Franklin had been there. Kinth then walks into his uncle's library, as Aldo and Enrico follow.

Sitting in his uncle's chair, he slowly spins around, examining the room. "I need to tell you two something before we leave here. And it's okay if you want to bow out of this after I say what needs to be said."

"Why would we bow out?" Aldo replies.

Leaning forward, Kinth rests his arms on the desk. "I'm just saying. I have no idea what's in store for us when we leave here."

Aldo glances at Enrico, who is now staring at the floor. He waits on whatever it is Kinth needs to say.

"Man, listen. We are out here breathing new air because of you. We could still be in that prison smelling piss and shit. So . . . spit it out, man," Aldo says.

Sighing, Kinth lets his head fall and then continues, "My father told me something before the battle at the island."

Aldo grabs one of the chairs in front of the desks that had been flipped over, turning it upright to sit. "What did he tell you?"

"Before my brother dethroned my father, and had him sent to the island, my father had a theory. One that he was slowly trying to prove."

"What was the theory?" Enrico asks, adjusting his stance as he leaned against the wall near the door. Slowly, some of the other prisoners entered the room, giving Kinth a larger audience.

"Our abilities are slowly killing us, some faster than others. Not only killing us, but aging us rapidly."

Aldo leans forward aggressively. "What?!"

Groans and grumbles fill the room.

"He wasn't able to prove it, but he developed a plan to begin investigating it. But my brother – the only Guardian that some of you know – found out about this theory and his plans. So, he had him removed."

"What was the plan?" Aldo asks.

"Uhmandra."

Aldo frowns. "A what?"

"It's an acronym –"

"What's an acronym?" someone asks.

Scratching the corners of his eyes, Kinth says, "Uh. A way to . . . shorten a bunch of words into one word. Or some shit like that," Kinth replies. "It stands for Human Designated Residential Area."

Enrico tries to make sense of the acronym, mouthing the words while using his fingers to count out the syllables.

Kinth notices Enrico's confusion. "Yeah I know. It didn't quite make sense to me either at first, but don't dwell on the word too much. He was trying his best to keep his plans hidden without complicating the process."

"Like hiding it in plain sight," Aldo interjects. "But what is it?"

"One of the ways my brother was able to dethrone my father was by assassinating his character. He spread false rumors that my father was sleeping around and impregnating women within the city. In actuality, my father was helping people get out of the city and moving them somewhere else. Most of these people were women who had or were carrying human children."

"Moved them, why?" A random prisoner joins in on the conversation.

"Because these people were human. His goal was to find all the humans left in the city and move them to a safe location. When my brother found out, he had his men counter my father's effort by kidnapping the humans they could find. Then, they moved them also. The good thing is, my father was able to move many to Uhmandra before he was found out. I don't know what came of the other humans. My guess is that they were killed."

"Where is Uhmandra?" Aldo asks.

"It's a hidden city. I'm not sure exactly."

Confused groans travel across the room.

Aldo scratches his head. "So you're saying that your father – the original Guardian – was secretly finding and transporting humans out of the city?"

"Yes."

"But why would that have been a problem? It sounds like your father was just trying to help," Enrico chimes in.

"My brother has always wanted more control. Control over others, over *things* . . . but never seemed to gain control over himself. My father's ideas made my brother fearful that my family would lose control over the city. And I'm sure he didn't like the idea of my father finding a way to help our city become normal. He loves his abilities. In fact, he uses them for evil more than good . . . If he has ever done anything good at all."

"What about this human everyone keeps talking about?" Aldo asks.

"I believe the human is somehow connected to all of this. He may have been one of the humans my father moved to safety. I don't know for sure. But how he and I met tells me that something much larger is going on out there. I need for y'all to understand that - if you continue this journey with me, there is no guarantee we will make it back."

The body language of the prisoners doesn't seem to change. Although, it is evident that some of them are concerned.

A loud bang rings from the front of the house. Someone was aggressively knocking on the front door. In a hurry, various prisoners scatter toward the front and the rear of the home, on edge.

As Kinth slowly makes his way out of the library and into the foyer, a voice speaks from the bottom of the front steps.

"Hey! We didn't mean to disturb, but we were hoping to have a word!" a man says.

Opening the door gradually, Kinth walks out onto the front porch. "What do you want?" In front of him stands a group of people of various ages and builds, men, and some women.

"I met an old man. I think this is his house," the man replies.

Kinth comes out a little further. "What you tellin' me this for?" He glances to his right. He can no longer see Miles and the others who had been headed toward the city. Aldo and some others follow behind Kinth outside.

"This man told me some things. He asked me some things, too, about missing people. My name is Jack, by the way."

Aldo quickly glances at Kinth. Returning the gaze, Kinth repositions his stance but says nothing.

Jack continues. "Um. Okay. Well . . . for some reason, that old man knew that people would be here looking for him. So, we are here to join your search party. Whatever it is that would have an old man out here alone with all the strange shit happening - has got to be important. Plus, we have had some of our own who have been attacked. Some of our people are also missing."

"Mmm hmm," Kinth groans suspiciously. "What did this old man look like?"

"Oh about yay high," Jack raises his hand into the air. "Long beard. Used a lot of big words. Spoke much different than I have heard in a while. Shit . . . maybe ever."

"Where do you think your people are?" Aldo tries to cut through the tension.

"It's not about what we think, it's what we know. Some of my people have seen some things. There are some mountains north and far east from here. Bodies are being dumped near them. Something is going on up them hills."

Freed prisoners, who had been listening to the conversation begin to groan and speak amongst themselves, disturbed by what Jack was saying. Kinth lowers his head, replaying the words as well.

Aldo approaches Kinth, with Enrico just behind him. "What you think?"

"Well, we can pretend like none of this shit is going on and go back to a life of uncertainty. We can also watch the same shit happen again to others. Or we can risk our lives to go find out what's going on, and maybe even save a few more in the process," Kinth replies, rubbing one of his sore arms.

"I like how this man thinks!" Jack yelps, with some of his people nodding in agreement.

Standing, Kinth approaches Jack. "My name is Kinth. This here is Aldo, and that's Enrico. These two, and those faces back there are my . . . family. More of my family is somewhere, but they're probably headed into danger. You come with us and we'll work together. One team; one focus. Find our people."

"Well, nice to meet you, Kinth. My name is Jack. I think I already I said that. But anyway. This bunch is *my* family. I have no problem with that at all."

"What are your abilities? What can y'all do?" Aldo chimes in, stepping forward.

Jack looks over his shoulder, giving an okay signal to his people to showcase their talents. Some within the group move objects across the ground telekinetically. Others control the natural elements, moving sand and weeds at will. A few can shapeshift into other beings completely.

"Nice," Kinth says. "We are going to need all the help we can find."

Chapter 20

THE GUARDIAN & TEAM - HOSTEL

"This place doesn't look like it has beds," The Guardian gawks, as he and his team gradually walk toward the recommended location where they could rest. Once there, they notice lights flickering through the cracks of the doors and windows. He scans the side of the building as they approach the front entrance. "I hope we didn't waste our time coming here. It's already been a long journey as it is."

"There are beds. But we may have to wait," the guard who recommended the place nervously responds.

As they approach the front of the dwelling, they observe the sandy roads and objects that protrude from the soil. Patrons come and go frequently, some falling over their feet in a drunken state. By this time, a small group of weary travelers have gathered near the entrance and are unable to enter.

One of The Guardian's men reaches out for the door. At this moment, someone from the staff pushes the door open from inside. "Get outta here! You silly fools! It was good to see y'all again. Peace and light." More patrons exit the venue. The staff member turns his attention to the travelers who have posted up on a stone wall nearby. "We have more room now since they left. Please come in."

The travelers make their way inside. Behind them, The Guardian and his men try to walk in as well. Only, they are stopped.

"Right now we are full. Some others should be leaving soon. Hang tight right over there," the employee says.

Grumbling, The Guardian walks where water would be, had the sand not grown so high in the area. He paces a path between objects that look like sand sculptures growing from the ground. Meanwhile, his men do the same near the same stone wall at which the other travelers were previously positioned.

Back inside the venue. Mathias is still standing and waiting on a response to his question.

"Can I sit down?" he asks once more. The first time he asked, his question was met with silence. Instead of waiting for an answer, he sits down next to the old man and sits across from Langston. "This paper . . . I find it interesting."

"I only see paper with words on it. Nothing too interesting about it to me," Langston replies.

Looking over the faces of everyone present, Mathias contemplates his next words. He places the paper in the center of the table. "Really, now? So if I told you that I was interested in finding some missing people, would you not find that interesting as well?"

"Alright, Mathias. Cut the crap!" the old man snaps, turning his body some to address Mathias directly.

Shock fills the eyes of Langston and Jesse. Talicia is not sure what to make of the conversation.

"I knew that was you," Mathias responds, smiling.

"You know this guy?" Langston interjects suspiciously.

Winston nods.

"Of course he knows me! My family once lived in Hock City. My father knew the first Guardian. This old guy right here was a very important person to The Guardian – and for that matter – to the city."

Langston listens before glancing over at Winston. Winston seems to involuntarily nod, further confirming that what Mathias was saying was true. Words that he had kind of already shared with Langston and Jesse, to some degree.

"What are you doing in these parts, Mathias?" Winston asks, just before raising his cup again.

Breathing in deep and then exhaling, Mathias glances over both his shoulders quickly before responding. "Okay. I see that I interrupted a serious discussion. So, let me get right down to it. The Guardian's son paid me a visit at Fetela."

"Who is this Guardian person?" Talicia finally speaks up after having been quiet for some time.

Mathias chuckles.

Turning almost to face her, Langston touches Talicia's hand gently. "The Guardian he is talking about – in power now - is an evil man. He runs Hock City, and apparently, he had people like me removed from it."

"Bingo!" Mathias exerts. "He had a lot of questions when he came to visit Fetela. One in which was about the people – like you – that he brought to me some cycles ago. He wanted to know what I did with them."

"What?!" The old man jerks around. "You have been trading . . . people?! Your father would be beyond disappointed in you, Mathias!"

"Can we back up? I don't understand." Langston says.

Grumbling, Winston clears his throat. "Mathias's father was one of many in other lands that used to do business with the original Guardian. Mathias took over for his father many, many cycles ago after his father became sickly."

"My father eventually died, and I have been running Fetela. And doing whatever I needed to ensure it kept standing," Mathias asserts himself sternly.

"But trading people?" Langston asks.

"I am not proud of some of our business. But we were desperate, and in need of many things. When Franklin came to me with his plans about those people, it meant my people could eat again."

"SO . . . you are the reason for my missing friends!" Talicia snaps, lunging at Mathias. "And for what happened to Langston!"

Talicia's actions startle Jesse, who had still been eating and drinking, causing him to spill some of his drink.

Mathias jolts backwards, dodging Talicia's grasp. "No, no, no, no. That's why I am here. I'm trying to figure out what is going on."

Grabbing Talicia by the waist, Langston does his best to calm her down before patrons really begin to notice the commotion. Some have glanced over but no hard stares yet.

Talicia's waitress friend returns, "Everything okay over here, girl?"

"Yeah. We fine."

The old man smiles at the waitress in a manner to shew her away before turning his attention back to Mathias. "Explain," he says.

"The humans that Franklin brought to me were exchanged for goods."

"Exchanged to whom?"

"A mysterious woman has been coming to Fetela specifically for the humans. I don't know her name."

Grumbling again, Winston replies, "Why not?"

"Before this moment, I didn't care what her name was. Recently she wouldn't tell me her name after I asked her for it. She was real . . . cryptic and defensive. Something is going on," Mathias continues.

"Something like what?" Langston asks.

"I don't know. But she's doing something with the humans. My team and I are headed to find out exactly. That's how we ended up here."

"Why all of a sudden do you care?" Talicia crosses her arms.

Shaking his head for a moment, Mathias sits back to scans their faces. "I don't want to be a part of it anymore. I was wrong, and I want to do whatever I can to fix it. I had tunnel vision. I was only thinking of my people instead of thinking about the bigger picture."

"And that would be . . .?" Winston glances over.

"I don't know. But I am open to finding out. Small rights to help fix big wrongs."

Frowning, Langston leans in and studies Mathias for a moment. "What's your plan?"

"The woman is expecting me to wait on her return. She promised to escort me to her base. Then, I could see for myself what she has been using the humans for. I don't trust her, so I decided that I would go to her. Hopefully, I can catch her off guard."

"You know where she is located?" Talicia directs her question to Mathias, but before he can reply, she jolts her body toward Langston excitedly. "Langston, this could be the place."

"Do you think going to this place with such a small group is wise?" the old man chimes in. "If this is indeed the place, there may be much more there to be of concern."

"I agree. Before noticing you here, my plan was to go in alone and have my people keep watch. I had only planned to observe."

"And then what?" Langston asks.

"Plan."

Talicia stands, speaking emotionally, "We don't have any more time to spare. No time to plan. I have been coming out here as often as I can, trying to gain any information I could find on where my friends are. I have been attacked and almost kidnapped myself. The fact that Langston is here, and you all are here with this information, tells me that I can no longer wait. *We* . . . can no longer wait. More people could be getting sent to this place. Please, tell us the direction."

At this moment, the sound of heavy footsteps and new conversations come from the front of the venue. Winston jerks around, looking at the group of men making their way inside the venue aggressively. "Oh no," he gasps.

"What? What is it?" Langston replies.

Glancing over his shoulders, Mathias responds, "He's here."

"Who?" Jesse finally speaks after having completely finishing his meal.

Looking over Mathias's shoulder, Langston can see The Guardian casually walking inside and examining the room. "The Guardian."

"We must leave at once!" Winston says worriedly.

Without saying a word, Talicia darts over Langston and runs into the kitchen. She has a quick conversation with her waitress friend and then bolts back to the table. "Quickly! Come! There are rooms available in the back. We can hide out."

Langston and Jesse hop to their feet. Mathias slides from underneath the table to let the old man out to follow behind the others, but he doesn't join them.

"What will you do?" Winston asks, stopping suddenly.

"I don't know. At the very least, buy us time to finish our talk," Mathias replies, giving the old man a quick wink.

Nodding, the old man quickly shuffles behind the others near the kitchen toward an adjacent hallway that lead to multiple staircases.

One of the members from Mathias' team jogs toward him. "You won't believe who just walked in," she says, out of breath.

"Yes. I know. I saw him."

"What do we do?"

Chapter 21

HOSTEL & THE FLATLANDS

EXHAUSTED, AND MAYBE A TAD BIT DELIRIOUS, THE Guardian doesn't take notice of the activity toward the rear of the venue by the kitchen. He was too focused on the commotion occurring at the venue's front entrance, taking place between other patrons. And so, he had missed the old man and the others skedaddle in the opposite direction.

Moments later, The Guardian and his men split up. They found places at which they could rest within various points throughout the large room. But still, they are unaware that their main purpose of traveling has just practically escaped before their eyes. Nor did they notice Mathias move to another location in the room, concealing his identity to observe and think. Another visit by The Guardian was not in his forecast.

"Come, come! This way!" The waitress waves at Talicia and Langston, before pointing to another door. "Only people who work here know of this room. It's where we come to nap sometimes between shifts. My boss is going to kill me if he finds y'all; so, please hide if you hear anything."

Nodding, Talicia runs into the room as Langston and Jesse quickly do the same. But the old man slows down and eventually stops. Jesse can feel the sudden quieting of footsteps behind him, causing him to turn around. "Why did you stop? C'mon!"

Langston overhears Jesse's plea and also stops. "What is it? What's wrong?"

Winston closes his eyes, breathing deeply before responding, "Go on ahead. I need to do something."

"Do what?" Langston replies.

"I need to send a message."

Langston frowns. "Huh?"

"Go on!" The old man waves Langston away. Then, he turns around and walks back through the kitchen toward the communal area.

Confused, Talicia chimes in, "What is he doing?"

Jesse looks around for a moment, dumbfounded. Shrugging at Talicia's question, Langston continues toward the hidden room behind her. Once inside the room, the waitress closes the door behind them. She then reconvenes her service duty.

Standing near the same table at which the group previously sat, the old man pauses for a moment. He notices Mathias tucked away, blending in with a random group of patrons. Shocked to see him, Mathias mouths something in a confused fashion toward the old man. *What is happening?* Mathias thinks.

Standing completely still, the old man closes his eyes again. He begins swaying a little, almost in a circular fashion, as if wind rapidly moved around him. Mouthing something to himself, he almost stumbles as he realizes what's happening.

"Hey! Gray man! You alright?" a random patron shouts from nearby.

First believing that the patron was speaking to someone else, Winston glances over his shoulders oddly. He quickly realizes that the patron didn't know his name. So, they were referring to his long, gray beard to get his attention. "Oh, oh. Yes. I am. Thank you, kindly."

Mathias continues to watch, waving his hand at Winston in disagreement. He does his best to instruct him to blend in. But the old man doesn't pay Mathias any mind. Instead, he begins to walk slowly toward the common area where The Guardian is sitting with his back turned. There he sits, talking amongst himself and his men.

Quickly, Mathias runs as fast as he can toward Winston, doing his best not to draw attention to himself. He grabs the old man by the arm, pulling him down into a nearby seat. "What are you . . .," Mathias lowers the octave of his voice, ". . . what are you doing?"

"Stalling," Winston replies, breathing heavily.

Mathias continues to scan the room. "Stalling? What do you mean? You're going to get us into some deep shit."

"I'm afraid, my son, that deep shit is inevitable at this point. But don't fret. I sent a message that will hopefully bring us some assistance."

"Assistance, huh? How are you so sure?"

The old man forms a smug smile.

"Well, what do we do to stall?" Mathias insists.

"We need to keep Franklin here by any means necessary."

Suddenly standing, The Guardian walks toward a nearby staircase. A few of his men are in tow. Mathias and the old man cover their faces enough to stay hidden, watching his movements.

"Where is he going?" Mathias thinks aloud.

"He must be staying for a while. Seems stalling won't be necessary for the moment. We still need to keep an eye on him. I know what he is searching for."

"I will stay here and alert my team. We will rotate shifts, so that we can all have a chance to get some sleep," Mathias says, keeping his face covered with his hands.

Patting Mathias on the shoulder, Winston says, "Good. My energy is dwindling. I will join the others and give them an update. Help will be here soon."

Having left his uncle's home, Kinth made his way across the nearby flatlands and lead what became an even larger group of focused allies. Despite hearing the news, as well as understanding the unpredictable nature of their journey and destination, the prisoners from the island faithfully walked with him. Not one person had left his side, but rather, they seemed to have grown more confident after reminiscing the fall of Delrusia Island.

The freed prisoners were also joined by the locals who accompanied Jack. Overall, it gave the group an even larger feeling of an oncoming victory regarding wherever they ended up. As of now, however, they weren't sure where they were going.

But Jack walks with purpose to the side of Kinth, with most of his people walking beside him closely. The two quietly share information with one another about their time in the Pines. Jack updates Kinth on what happened at the Exchange, as well as the events causing his friend Eli to go missing. He goes on to share more information about the visit by Kinth's uncle. Then, he elaborates more on what he knows about the area where he believes some of his friends are.

From the outside looking in, Jack's group appears harmless. But in actuality, many of his people possess abilities where, if these were combined, they could pose a serious threat to their adversary. It's much like the Ekladi people who are also traveling with the group.

Kira kept up her side of the bargain, having already relayed a message for some of her other people to join Kinth. They would meet them at a certain marker within the hills.

Aldo and Enrico are spread out amongst the remaining freed prisoners, talking amongst themselves. Because of a breeze, they keep a close eye to the harsh sway of foliage and ensure that it wasn't a disguised threat. The color changes, as the darkening of the sky has them on edge.

As the large group moves across the hills, the number of its members grows. Apparently, news has traveled throughout this part of the Pines. Mostly it's because of Jack's doing. He prepped as many people as he could before he left, informing these people of his plan. Still, he was unsure whether he could persuade an alliance with Kinth; or anyone for that matter. The old man told Jack some details about Kinth, but not much. Jack used this information to find him. His only goal: to find his missing friends.

Before his arrival to North Hock, Jack had searched more for Eli. He even told other friends and associates his plans, based on his discussion with the old visitor. After visiting Eli's home, where he discovered that not only was Eli and his family gone - but also many others, Jack was motivated to do more.

In the middle of their conversation, Kinth trembles and grabs his head with both hands. Groaning, he stops abruptly and falls to one knee. An unexpected pain travels across his head, as if something was trying to penetrate his skull.

Noticing his actions, the large group immediately forms a circle around Kinth and Jack. Aldo and Enrico run over worriedly to investigate.

"Watch the perimeters!" Aldo shouts, before kneeling next to Kinth. "What is it, man?"

"You alright there, buddy?" Jack interjects, seemingly just as concerned as everyone else.

Breathing heavily with a mixture of groans and mumbles, Kinth shakes his head before standing. "I know where they are!"

"What?" Aldo replies anxiously.

"My uncle and the others. I know where they are."

Jack scratches his face, perturbed. "Now how in the world do you know their location all of a sudden?"

Enrico's and Aldo's expressions reverberate Jack's statement.

Taking his time to respond, Kinth continues to walk again. Though, this time, Kinth walks more rapidly. "We need to hurry. My uncle has sent me a message mentally."

"Say what?" Aldo exclaims, doing his best to keep up with Kinth's pace. "Kinth, man! Hold up!"

At the moment, all eyes and ears are fixated on Kinth. Everyone awaits an explanation. "My uncle has the ability to communicate with me mentally. He sent me snapshots of his location."

"Snapshots?"

"Yeah . . . like abstract pictures. Like when you move pass something quickly but try to remember what you saw. I believe he showed me the route that they took and where they are. It looks like a rest stop with food and ale. It's been a long time since he has communicated with me like this. So, we need to hurry before I lose the visions."

Aldo comes in a little closer to whisper, "Is the human there too?"

Kinth nods. "And danger is closing in on them."

"Then we need to find a way to move faster," Enrico says distinctly. "We won't make it in time at our current pace."

Having had kept a close eye on the group's movement and listening to every word, the Ekladi members subtly approach the conversation. "Allow us to assist," one of the members says humbly.

"Assist how?" a random prisoner responds.

Wondering the same thing, Kinth slows his pace to acknowledge the offer. "What do you propose?"

"Some of us can control the elements. I'm sure there are others who can do the same," the young Ekladi woman says. Her voice grows louder, in an effort to be heard. "We can use the sand to move us quickly."

"This is something you all have done before?" Kinth crosses his arms.

"Yes. We can also hide within the sand so that it looks like the remnants of a storm. We should be able to cut our travel time in half if we all work together."

Kinth scans the area quickly. "Mmm, hmm."

"But there is one downside."

"Which is . . . ?" Kinth replies.

"Visibility is low when we do this. We may lose some from your group. Normally it is just my people doing this. We have a . . . chemistry about us. Most of you are strangers to us. So, we can't guarantee -"

"Guarantee what? That we will live through this?" Kinth interjects, his tone growing impatient. "Let's just do it. Quickly. Before something finds us out here."

Without speaking, the young woman nods. Quickly she approaches her people, shouting moments later, "Those who can control the elements, please help us form a circle around the others!"

Various other people — prisoners, and strangers who had recently joined the journey follow her orders. They move toward the outskirts of the group. Locking their arms so they could use their hands, all closed their eyes and dug deep within themselves. Therefore, they could bring forth their abilities.

At first, some in the group struggle, since they have adapted to working alone while using their abilities. But after a few moments of erratic winds, the group finally moves the sand and soil. It slowly moves the group across the ground, as if a platform with wheels were beneath of them.

"We need to move faster!" Kinth shouts. "C'mon! We might as well be walking at this pace!"

Noticing some wild, six-legged creatures moving about the lands, a random woman from the group speaks up. "I have another idea!"

Chapter 22

HAKRA & FEEZA – LAB, IFERA HOSPITAL

"EVERYBODY OUT!" Hakra shouts, having grown even more frustrated with the news his Cepha scout provided. "Now! Leave me with Feeza. You may reenter to continue your testing shortly."

Startled by the sudden outburst, the technicians drop what they had been doing. All jog toward the lab doors, forcing themselves through the exit before the doors opened completely. The old woman follows behind them hesitantly, her face filled with concern.

Frozen by the tone of his voice, Niandres trembles before finally snapping out of his fearful gaze. He, too, follows behind the old woman.

"WAS I NOT CLEAR?! MOVE!" Hakra yells again, pacing rapidly around the lab environment while pushing buttons and moving levers. Clearly he knows his way around the lab beyond giving orders.

"Hakra . . . what's . . . what's wrong?" Feeza stammers, fearful of the swift change in his demeanor.

Glancing over his shoulder to ensure that he and Feeza were alone, Hakra continues his actions. "Look around you, Feeza. What do you see?"

"Umm. Equipment. Testing. People. All elements to further your plans," Feeza stammers more. The exhaustion of her dealings with Hakra begin to show through her body language.

"No! The future! Liberation! Preservation!"

Feeza gently pulls out one of the few chairs in the room, sitting quietly. Lowering her head, she continues to listen.

"At some point along the way, it seems that you have forgotten the importance of what I am trying to accomplish here. Even I am but just a small portion of something much, much larger."

"Hakra —"

"Shh. Quiet."

A harsh silence grips the room.

Hakra walks slowly toward Feeza, kneeling and placing his fingers on Feeza's chin to lift her head. "Do you believe me? Do you . . . trust me?" Hakra asks, affectionately, after making intense eye contact.

Feeza pulls her head away. "I think it would be best for me to get some sleep. Then, I can return to Mathias on time. If I do not show up within a reasonable time frame, he may try to find me."

Saying nothing, Hakra studies Feeza's face for a moment. He gives such an intense stare that it feels like the room's air had been suddenly sucked out of it. Then, he stands to his feet and returns to one of the nearby workstations.

Standing, Feeza begins to walk slowly toward the exit. "What will you do about all this? Do you need my assistance with anything?"

"Tell me, Feeza. Do you remember how we met?" Hakra looks at a clipboard with several items of data written on it. He scans the paperwork quickly, almost machine-like.

"You know I do, Hakra. What kind of question is that?"

"Well, then. I expect for you to reflect on that a little more from this point forward. By doing that, maybe it will help you with your decision-making and your judgement." Hakra quickly pulls down on another lever connected to a wide panel. At this moment, the subjects inside of the cylinders – some wearing hospital gowns with tubing and wires connected at various points of their bodies - within the center of the lab begin to moan and scream. The various lighting inside of the tube above them grow brighter. Some of it traveled rapidly to the apex of the room, where the tube connected to the ceiling.

Startled by the unexpected sound of screams and noisy working equipment, Feeza quickly left the room. Lab workers reentering the space rushed by her as they came into the lab. But this time, they were accompanied by a group of larger workers.

Hakra watches Feeza exit the lab closely. Once she is out of his view, he turns to a pair of guards who had been standing in the shadows the entire time. Saying nothing, Hakra nods at them. Both nod in return and leave the lab through a different exit.

"Shall we continue?" a small lab worker says.

"Yes. But first . . . come get these few subjects!" Hakra shouts over his shoulder. "They didn't provide much!"

Sighing deeply, he walks over to one of the subjects. He stands directly in front of the cylinder before it opened. Inside of the cylinder is a tall, muscular creature with a slim, but athletic human-like body. The creature hasn't any eyes. Instead, he has a thick layer of skin that moves where human eyes would be.

The cylinder makes a sound. Then, oxygen releases before it opens. Large lab workers stand nearby as the smaller technicians remove the wiring connected to the subject's body. After removing this wiring, the subjects fall limp to the floor. Some have fluids oozing from their bodies. Quickly stepping forward, the lab workers grab these subjects by their limbs. Then, they toss them inside another tube that's extended well below the platform, similar to that of a trash chute.

"Retrieve them as normal and take them to the dump site!" a tiny, elderly man with thick goggles says. He pushes a button that seals the tube, sending the unconscious subjects downward.

Meanwhile, the larger lab workers are evidently kept around for muscle. They say nothing to the instructions as they leave the room.

At this point, Feeza has rushed back to the main level of the building. She moves quickly out another set of doors, going toward a new section of the hospital that leads to her living quarters in an adjacent building. A long, glassed hallway is in this section. She pauses here to look out at the other areas which could be seen around the facility. These included a dark, eerie area just off to the back of a mountain that housed the lab testing. Walking in a straight line toward this area on a graveled path are the large lab workers. All are doing what they had done many times before: bringing unconscious - and for some, dead subjects - to this dump site. Therefore, they could be disposed of by creatures lurking in the area.

Between the workers are metal containers on wheels. The bodies of test subjects are piled to capacity, being pulled, or pushed by the workers. At a certain point, the workers disappear into the darkness.

I can't . . . I can't continue this, Feeza thinks. Quickly she continues toward her living quarters. It was just a couple turns down multiple hallways. Inside her living area, which was a small office that was essentially gutted to create one large living space, she sat on the edge of her bed contemplating.

Feeza pauses, taking a moment to reflect on her turbulent time as a scout for Hakra, her boss. But more importantly . . . he was her savior. There had been long journeys, close encounters and a few times she had to fight for her life. Her mind flashes, with thoughts moving about regarding her youth. When she was just a teen, Hakra had rescued her from a group of women who had been luring young girls into a harrowing life of sex trafficking. Hakra had been on a mission for new subjects himself. But then, he discovered Feeza being held captive in a lounge's basement. She was the only one of the group of girls he spared, using the others as test subjects.

Shaking her head to rid herself of the thoughts, Feeza quickly moves about her room. She grabs various things, throwing them into a vintage women's backpack. She darts toward the door but stops abruptly, placing her hand on her face. Then, she thinks a bit more about what she was about to do.

Outside, the large lab workers move along the dark path, which looked like a spec from Feeza's view. They ascend the inside of the mountain behind the testing facility. This mountain had been carved in such a way to provide a secret path to various exits, thereby bringing test subjects in and out discreetly. At the end of one of these paths is a large pit, positioned just before the flatland hills and a long road that winds in the distance.

Inside the pit walked gruesome-looking, large, scorpion-like hybrid creatures. From the chest upward they appear like humans, but have scorpion-like features everywhere else. These creatures move slowly around the pit, as if they are waiting on a delivery, and feed on the random bodies that fill the open space. As the lab workers close in, they're met by groans, screams and other anguishing sounds - both subtle and loud. Some subjects have awakened and do their best to fight their way to the edge of the pit. They climb the walls, but then meet their demise at the hands of the scorpion creatures.

Chapter 23

LANGSTON, JESSE, WINSTON & OTHERS – HOSTEL

NOISES COMING FROM THE DINING HALL OF THE HOSTEL sound as if someone is trying to bottle muffled and sporadic conversations. Langston leans against a wall, while sitting on one of the beds in the room. He listens to as much as he can. At times, he glances over at Jesse who lies on his back. Jesse stares at the ceiling. Having grown tired after eating, Jesse yawns a bit. Talicia sits on the floor in-between Langston's legs, leaning back on him and wondering about everything that was said only moments before. She wasn't expecting to run into Langston, let alone this turn of events.

Sitting up, Langston startles Talicia as he's alerted by the squeak of the secret door. Someone was opening it.

"It's okay, everyone. It's just me," Winston says, feeling his way around the room before slowly sitting down in a chair.

"What are we going to do? We can't stay in here forever," Talicia crosses her legs.

Standing, Langston begins to pace around the room slowly. "I need to get home."

Jesse turns over, lying on his side to see everyone.

"What about what that guy told us? What about our friends?" Talicia looks up and over her shoulder, clearing her throat. "We can't go home yet."

Langston jerks around, his eyebrows raised. "Why not?"

Talicia exhales deeply, leaning forward and resting her arms on her legs. "We can't go back home. That's part of the reason why I am here. I started looking for you and the others, going back home when I could. But whoever has been kidnapping people found out about our home. Somehow, they found out that some of the people there were special - like you."

"What do you mean? Are you saying that there are others there like me? Wait . . . are you – are you human, too?"

Winston clears his throat aggressively. "Young Langston," he says.

"What?!" Langston replies, turning around to face the old man.

"Shh. Shh. Not too loud, please. I need to concentrate and we don't want anyone to hear us back here."

Startled by Langston's tone, Jesse sits up on the bed.

Winston continues. "I guess I need to finish telling you what you need to know, especially while I have the energy. Your home is a special place called Uhmandra, created by the only Guardian that I honor. Langston, you are one of many that the original Guardian tried to protect."

"I don't understand."

"The Guardian created a secret place where he hid you and others like you. His goal was to keep you all there. With time, he would begin to investigate a way for those with abilities to return to their human state. But once his ideas became known, there was pushback. So, he had to implement his plan in secrecy. Instead of giving an order for someone else to do this, he went out on his own. He gathered up as many as he could to find who were like you. He explained the benefits to your mother and other parents. She believed in what he wanted to do. You were very young during this time."

"Who else knows about this? About my home?" Langston asks.

"I can't say for certain," Winston says, pausing for a moment and stroking his beard. "Franklin may know some, because he has been suspicious for a while. The original Guardian didn't mention the word Uhmandra to anyone. Except, he did mention it to members of his counsel. As far as I know, I am the only surviving member. I haven't told anyone else until this moment."

Talicia scratches her head. "This is too much. Somebody else knows, and has been taking our friends!" she continues, sternly.

"Langston, I agree with your friend. Going home may not be wise just yet."

"What would you have me do?"

Leaning in a bit closer, Winston replies, "Stay the course."

Flopping down onto the bed, Langston lies down and says nothing more. Talicia affectionately joins him, lying by his side.

"Get some rest, everyone. We will figure this out!" the old man says.

A while later, Langston begins to wake up. He rubs his face and eyes gently. He can see the old man in his peripheral asleep. Cocking his head up a little, he notices Jesse asleep nearby. Feeling the bed beside him, he realizes that Talicia is gone. Sitting up quickly, Langston causes a piece of paper to fall from his lap to the floor. The paper, a flyer, had been in Talicia's possession. But something was written on the back of it:

Langston, I couldn't sleep. I decided to go and see if I could find more information that might help us. I am glad that you are okay. If you are okay, maybe our friends are, too. I hope to see you again soon.

Langston frowns as he reads the paper, causing lines to grow in his face. Becoming more upset, he anxiously runs from the room without waking the old man or Jesse. Standing just outside of the door, he scans the dining area of the hostel. There's neither a sign of Talicia, nor her waitress friend. He runs toward the front entrance, passing Mathias in a corner, who had dozed off.

Seemingly getting through the crow unnoticed, Langston pushes the front doors open and jogs outside. As he looks to his left and his right, still there's no sign of Talicia.

"Shit!" he says loudly.

Sounds of footsteps grow from the sides of Langston.

"Aww, what's wrong? All alone?" a familiar voice says.

Jolting around, Langston back steps away from the voice. The Guardian was standing near him. Langston walks backwards quickly before bumping into one of The Guardian's men who had quietly snuck up behind him. Slowly, Langston is being surrounded.

The Guardian grins evilly. "I didn't believe my tracker when he told me that he thought he smelled you. But I guess that's why he will always be a better tracker than me. After all, look what we found! Happy to see me?"

Langston tries to run off. But then, he is quickly grabbed and held tightly by one of The Guardian's men. He tries his best to break free, saying nothing.

"For a moment, I was almost in bed with a pretty thing when he picked up a familiar scent. I couldn't believe it. How did we get so lucky? We thought we had lost you again somewhere out in these fields when we discovered . . .," The Guardian snaps his fingers, ". . . this pretty little number leaving."

Another one of The Guardian's men comes from the side of the venue, holding Talicia tightly by the arm.

Langston's eyes grow wide. "Talicia!"

"Get off me, you beast!" Talicia says, before noticing Langston being held similarly. "Oh no! Langston! I'm so sorry! I'm so sorry. I don't know what I was thinking."

Crossing his arms, The Guardian steps between the two, saying, "Shh, shh, shh. Who else is with you in there? The kid? My sister?" He places his forefinger over his lips, thinking deeply.

"You should be more concerned about who is with him out here!" A new voice joins the conversation. The voice travels downward onto the group.

The Guardian's mouth gradually opens in shock, as he looks around and then upward. "What – what are you doing here?"

With one leg up on the roof's edgework, Mathias leans on his thigh casually. "You know what's funny? We were just talking about you, and suddenly, here you are."

"Kill him!" The Guardian shouts without hesitation, after having noticed Mathias. "Take the human and the girl and get outta here!"

Attempting to run away, The Guardian's men are met by a wall of Mathias's people.

Mathias still watches from the roof, smiling, "Au, contraire, my friend!"

"Yep! Contraire is right, brother! You're not going anywhere!" Another, more aggressive sounding voice has joined in on the discussion.

The Guardian turns quickly to see who was there, but then, his confidence shrinks in fear. "It . . . it can't be!"

Riding the backs of large desert creatures, Kinth and the others with him move briskly down a neighboring hill. "Let's go!" Kinth yells to the others. All acknowledge his order with various yells of agreement. The size of the group has increased, and are coming from various directions over the mountainous hills.

Having mutated partially, The Guardian readies himself as the first layer of Kinth's group charges at him. The Guardian, with anger in his eyes at seeing his brother, gracefully maneuvers himself to avoid being harmed. He immobilizes each person crossing his path.

Adjacently, Mathias makes his way down from the roof. He moves closer toward The Guardian, hoping to free Langston and his friend. He jumps, ducks and moves quickly, fighting his way closer while the various people from both sides clash.

Back inside, Jesse awakens. He notices that Langston and Talicia are gone. So, he runs over to their bed to inspect it, as if they were still in the room hiding. Running back toward the old man, Jesse grabs him aggressively.

"Wake up! They're gone! Wake up!" Jesse says to Winston frantically.

Startled, Winston clears his throat insistently before responding, "What? What is it?!"

"They're gone!"

"Who?" the old man says before cocking his head to look over Jesse's shoulder. "Oh. Oh no."

Jesse darts out of the room, without saying anything more.

"Wait! Wait a minute!" Winston shouts out. "These young people will be the death of me."

Briskly moving around the crowded dining area, Jesse makes it to the front entrance of the venue. He bursts out onto the sandy walkway. His eyebrows raise when he witnesses a scene he had somewhat seen before: a large group of people were battling in front of him. But his shock is neither of the fight nor the amount of people. Instead, his shock comes from the fact that Kinth was at the center of it all. He didn't think he would ever see him again.

Still being held tightly by one of The Guardian's larger team members, Langston shouts out, "Jesse! Get back!" He, as well as Talicia, are gradually being pulled away.

"Oh no!" Winston says, shuffling up onto the heels of Jesse, while noticing what was happening.

"We gotta do something!"

Winston stammers a bit as he traverses his thoughts, but doesn't respond to Jesse's sentiments right away. Feeling a different energy nearby, he observes an adjacent hill. Winston stares at the landscape for a moment. There he notices the silhouette of someone standing at the hill's peak. The person's cloak flaps in the wind. Studying the person for a moment, he can't seem to move because of what he sees. Winston closes his eyes briefly and then reopens them, nodding at the person up on the hill.

Chapter 24

THE FIGHT - HOSTEL

STANDING AT THE HILL'S APEX IS FEEZA. HAVING USED ONE of her abilities, she has teleported short distances to move quickly from Ifera to the battle near the hostel. Her initial destination was Fetela, with the hopes to catch Mathias before he left. But she was able to feel some of the strange vibrations in the distance. The rumble of movement produced by many caused her to become curious and change course.

Patiently observing, Feeza watches for a moment. She notices the many layers of odd creatures and people crowding the small area near the hills of the hostel. All are clashing for unknown reasons. Her first instinct is to return to Hakra and inform him of the subjects she has found - an almost robotic, programmed reaction. But she shakes off these thoughts and sticks to her change of heart. She can no longer support Hakra's mission.

Her next thought was on what to do, since she was certain Mathias was within this group. She had noticed some familiar faces from her last visit to Fetela. But who else is amongst the battle? Even with her abilities, she was no match by herself for the various threats moving about at the bottom of the hill.

But then, she notices someone exiting the building behind what appeared to be a child. An older man. For some reason, his presence calms her. Without notice, she feels the older man's presence as if he is standing right near her.

"Look out," the voice says softly in her mind.

Unexpectedly, Feeza opens her eyes - only to be met by a small group of wild, desert creatures. They are running full speed in her direction, with gruesome teeth and wicked smiles. Thinking quickly, Feeza teleports quickly in various directions. At each endpoint, she stabs the creatures and kills them.

Regaining her breath, she looks back at the old man from the distance and nods. The old man nods back. She then scans the area more before breathing in deeply. At the moment of her exhale, she clasps her hands together aggressively. She does this in such a way that she sends strong, sonic vibrations in the direction of the battle at hand.

The vibration moves through the soil and sand, traveling all the way to the core of the battle. Thus, the force of it results in a quake powerful enough that it causes the hills and anything nearby to shake. Those still on the backs of creatures fall to the ground. Despite being entangled and throwing blows at one another, Kinth, The Guardian and others by the venue stumble as well. Patrons who were once inside the hostel anxiously exit the building. They run as best as they can toward various hills.

Feeza smiles a little while moving in closer. The once merciless crowd of both hybrid man and creature are preoccupied with the aftereffects of the quake. It had been a while since she had used this specific ability, and she was proud that she wasn't as rusty as she expected. "Enough!" She shouts, "You are fighting the wrong enemy!"

Struggling to their feet, The Guardian and his men gather themselves.

"Who are you?!" The Guardian turns his attention to Feeza from a distance, yanking himself from Kinth's grasp.

"This isn't finished, brother," Kinth interjects, propping himself onto one knee.

The Guardian scoffs and replies, "I just can't get rid of you."

Across the way, Mathias manages to position himself in the path Feeza walks, "I know who she is!" he asserts, walking toward her. "It's strange to see you here."

"I have information for you. I was headed to your home when I felt a lot of energy coming from this direction. Quickly, please – move inside!" Feeza examines the area, attempting to get everyone's attention as she approaches the venue's entrance. "I will tell you more indoors. Please."

Standing slowly, Kinth dusts himself off and glances at Aldo. "We can't all fit in that place," he says aloud.

"Kinth, you know this woman?" Jack takes a step forward.

"I hope you do, Kinth, cause damn she sexy!" Aldo strokes his chin, scanning Feeza from head to toe.

Rolling her eyes, Feeza replies, "Well, if we all can't fit, pick a representative for your groups and come inside. Quickly!"

"Aldo, you hold down the fort out here with Enrico and our new friend Jack-"

"No. We need to be in there watching your back," Aldo interjects.

Clearing his throat, Jack agrees. "Sorry, buddy. But I, too, think I need to be in there. I need to hear what this pretty miss has to say for myself. Just for the sake of my people, of course."

"We concur," a random Ekladi person steps forward.

Sighing, Kinth glances at the hills, "Okay."

"There is a cave nearby. My people can show everyone the way, should you want to rest there," Mathias adds.

"Mmm. I think we are better right here, stranger," Aldo replies.

Quietly making his way closer, Winston approaches his nephews. Meanwhile, Jesse, Langston and Talicia stand closely behind him.

"Well, I didn't expect this sort of reunion," the old man says.

Looking over the old man's shoulder, The Guardian chuckles to himself after noticing Langston. "See you inside," he says, winking.

Once back inside of the venue, those who had been already noticed had mostly cleared out. Because of the quake Feeza caused, most of the patrons had left in a hurry. So, only the wait staff was left behind.

Talicia quickly runs toward her friend, who had been cowering behind tables in a corner the entire time. Both talk amongst themselves.

Everyone else positions themselves at various tables, sitting with the group in which they were a member.

Winston, Mathias, Kinth, Langston and Jesse sit together. Aldo and Enrico sit nearby. Others from their perspective groups line the walls and other tables.

Feeza paces between the tables, waiting on everyone to quiet down.

"Who are you?!" a random person from Jack's group shouts unexpectedly.

Pausing, Feeza quickly reviews her decision regarding Hakra's betrayal. There was no going back. "My name is Feeza. I come from the mountains of Dyadika. From the office of Hakra at Ifera."

"So," someone else says, growing frustrated.

Talicia quickly glances at Langston with a stunned look.

"Many of you have had members of your family, friends and communities go missing. Yes?"

An uproar of anger and confusion grows within the room. Several people stand and begin shouting their resentments at Feeza. Some throw various objects from tables just before the old man stands and makes his way toward her.

"Please! Please! Let's calms ourselves so this woman can say what she needs to say!" Winston pleads.

"Shut up, old man!" a large creature with a thick neck says. He throws a cup filled with ale toward Winston.

Before the cup could reach him, Winston closes his eyes momentarily. He uses his ability to suspend the cup in the air as its contents escape. When he opens his eyes, there is a line of ale in the air, with the cup at the end. "Come, now. There is no need for that," Winston says.

Because of the old man using his ability, the room grows silent.

At this moment, Winston beings to stumble some and nearly falls. Langston rushes to his side with Kinth on his heels. Both grab the old man and bring him back to their table. The cup that had been suspended in the air continues its route, dropping to the floor by Feeza.

The Guardian grins evilly from where he is sitting.

"What's wrong, uncle?" Kinth asks quietly.

"Yeah. What's *wrong*, uncle?" The Guardian says evilly.

Shaking his head, the old man waves off the question. "I'm okay. I'm okay."

Across the room, Feeza continues, "You have every right to be angered. I may very well be responsible for your missing people."

"We should kill you where you stand!" a voice yells from the rear of the room.

"While I deserve that, you wouldn't get the information I am about to share with you if you do."

Jack repositions himself in his seat, glancing at the floor as he listens. "So those bounty hunters at The Exchange - the ones who attacked my friend. They're with you?" he asks.

"No. I work alone, mostly . . . for a man by the name of Hakra."

Winston's eyes widen as shock fills his face.

"For most of my adult life, I have been a scout for Hakra. My job has been to find people with unique abilities."

Mathias drops his head shamefully. Then, he glances at The Guardian.

"Find them, and then what?" Enrico asks.

Feeza lowers her gaze and bites her bottom lip subtly. "Testing and extraction."

More grumbles and moans of disagreement ensue.

"For what purpose?" Kinth's deep voice silences everyone. He stands and crosses his arms.

"To be liberated from death. To live forever."

Aldo finishes chugging a cup of ale, "What the hell does that mean?"

"It means that Hakra has been taking the abilities from individuals and using them to create a way to live forever."

The Guardian crosses his legs, leaning back onto the table in a casual fashion. "So, if I may, you are saying that people are being sacrificed? Is that correct, pretty lady?"

Shamefully, Feeza looks away and says nothing.

Her demeanor causes a brief uproar, right before shouting could be slightly heard through the walls. A weapon discharges, alerting everyone to a new fight beginning outside. Everyone within the room grows alert.

The Guardian and his men quickly stand, as Mathias and his group does the same.

A few aisles over, Kinth tilts his head slowly. He observes the behavior in the room. He wasn't prone to acting quickly without processing situations carefully.

Winston leans in toward Langston and Jesse. "You two need to hide. Now!" He does his best to whisper. "Go, now, back to that room. It is growing unsafe here."

"Why?" replies Jesse.

Aldo, Enrico, Jack, and the others have all become alert to the quiet conversation.

Langston leans toward the old man in the same fashion. "Are you sensing something? What if we get trapped in that room?"

"We won't," says Talicia. "There's an exit in the room that leads to the other side of the hills behind this place."

"Go! Go now!"

Noticing the eyes of his allies nearby, Kinth says, "He is the only human in the room. There are many threats in here. But something tells me that the real threat is out those doors."

At this point, all eyes are fixated on the front doors of the venue.

Chapter 25

HOCK CITY – THE EARLY DAYS

MANY CYCLES BEFORE THE PRESENT, THE ORIGINAL Guardian would have regular council meetings as he saw fit. The purpose of these meetings involved discussing important topics such as the overall care and security of the city, as well as its goals and troubles. In an empty, aging warehouse, these meetings would take place in a concealed, back room. It was just a few paces from the front entrance, in what appeared to be the manager's office.

Oftentimes, Winston, The Guardian's closest family and confidant, would be the first to arrive to these meetings. He would scan the area, based on his own recognizance. Winston wanted to ensure that no threats were present -

man, creature or otherwise. Though, on this particular day, Winston was surprised at whom were already in the meeting area and awaiting his arrival.

Startled by the subtle sound of whispers, Winston entered the room. Slowly he approaches the large, rickety table positioned in the center. "What are you two doing here already? The meeting is –"

"We know when the meeting is, uncle," Franklin says arrogantly. "What are YOU . . . doing here this early?"

"Well I . . . I always come a bit early at the request of your father, Franklin. We are living in turbulent times. So, I am just looking out for this city's best interest."

"Oh, really? You don't think we have this *city's* . . . best interest in mind as well?"

"Enough of this shit!" The other person sitting at the table bangs his fist on the table, before leaning on it. The evil in his eyes is almost electric. "Get to the point, Franklin."

Clearing his throat, Franklin leans forward and rests an arm on the table. "You are well aware, uncle, of what we discussed. So, I am going to ask you again . . . Are you with us? Because my patience in growing thin."

"I have already told you, nephew, that I am not interested in your position. My loyalty rests with your father and to this city. My loyalty rests within the good, not with –"

"Oh, save me the speech!" Franklin stands quickly and begins to slowly pace around the table. He fingers at the drawer handles of old cabinets that line the wall. "His ideas will end this place. It will make us weak compared to the other territories!"

Winston sighs deeply, looking up toward the ceiling as if his next thoughts lived there. "How do you know about his ideas?"

"We hear things," Hakra chimes in.

"Lies! I won't stand here and be a part of this."

"I'm going to ask you one last time . . . Are you with us? Will you join us in keeping this wonderful city alive, with its beauty of man and creatures combined? Together, they provide us strength. Strength that we can use to be powerful forever. Power that will allow us to slowly consume the other realms threatening our existence. To do away with weakness, uncle, and be fervent forever!"

Walking slowly towards his nephew, an expression of sadness fills Winston's face. "What has become of you, child? This thirst of control. I know your youth was a rough one, but this is not you. This is not what your father has fought so hard for. He didn't want to see you turn into this."

"Ha! You . . . you don't know me. My own father doesn't even know me! He has spent most of his time catering to the well-being of Kinth and Shaida, so much so that I was like a fixture on the wall. Spare me."

Hakra slams his full palm on the table. The table caves in some, leaving a deep hand print. "QUIET! I could care less about your family dealings."

"And you . . . have no shame? Just as I, you sit as a member of this council. This table is sacred. Our Guardian confides in us. He trusts us to help him lead this city. Will you betray him as well?"

Hakra reaches toward his lapel, unpinning a small button. He places the button on the table, sliding it toward Winston. "This is not a betrayal. Consider this my resignation."

Tension grows within the room, bringing forth an unnerving level of silence.

"What are you'll planning? Please, tell me it's not violence. We have enough of that in this city. Please!"

"I feel sorry for you, uncle. Following that man so blindly," Franklin says as he exits the room. "Don't fall with him."

Saying nothing, Hakra looks at Winston with a straight face before leaving behind Franklin. Outside the warehouse, Hakra stops walking to observe the activities around him. "Our deal still stands, no matter what," he says with a whisper.

"Yeah. Why wouldn't it?" Franklin replies, keeping his body facing the road in front of them. He watches the activity of various people nearby.

Before saying anything more, Hakra studies Franklin's demeanor which seemed unsettling to him. After adjusting his clothing a bit, he approaches Franklin. Standing right by his side, he says, "I get the old hospital in the mountains and everything in it. Plus, I get a portion of the city's technology."

"And you will help me become Guardian of this city. I get to use your resources whenever I please. When your testing shows promise, I want to be next in line."

Hakra nods and Franklin does the same. The two walk off in different destinations.

Back inside the warehouse, Winston walks slowly toward one of the chairs near the table. After turning it around, he falls backwards into the chair, stunned by the exchange of words only moments ago. He rests his arm on the table and pauses, as he looks at the handprint Hakra left. *How has he become so powerful?* Winston thinks. Thereafter, Winston changes his thoughts. He reflects on how life was just after the events that changed everything in Pineville.

The original Guardian was one of the first people in his neighborhood to step up and begin planning ways to get his community back to normal. Each day, before the sky began changing, he would set up several milk crates and boxes along the sidewalk in front of his house. These crates and boxes were filled with things he and his wife decided they no longer needed. They included certain canned goods, clothing, utensils, and technology and more.

TAKE SOMETHING, LEAVE SOMETHING one of the signs said that he placed at one end of the row of boxes. WE HAVE TO HELP EACH OTHER TO GET THROUGH THIS, another sign said at the other end. More people would come each day. News spread of a place where supplies could be found. Sometimes, people would come and knock on his door directly before he had the chance to wake up and get his goods outside.

"Hey man! We came to hock some stuff. Or trade if you got anything," a small man with his family said one morning.

This went on for days as the darkness in the sky became unpredictable. At times, people were scared to come outside. But the trading of goods continued and grew in size, with other people in various neighborhoods participating. This effort would form into The Exchange - a large, open-area bartering environment.

Nearby, construction took place to create a small, protected city. The idea was to create a place that was far enough away from the object. It seemed to be harming and changing the environment. The city would be enclosed and protected by tall walls.

Because of his efforts to help his fellow neighbors, The Guardian was named the leader of this city before it even had a name. Winston was chosen as his second-in-command, mostly because he was trusted family. Also, it was because of his balanced and logical thinking. But he refused to move from his home and into the city, citing that things would be fine where he was.

The old man quickly snaps out of his thoughts, realizing that he had briefly fell into a deep meditation of reflection. He missed the old times. Sometimes, he had trouble staying in the present whenever he would become stressed. As he comes to himself, he regains coherence and notices that everyone is at alert in the dining area of the hostel. Langston is still waiting on a response from him.

"What is it?" Langston says.

Winston gently pushes Langston. "Go while you can!"

"Langston, come on!" Talicia says, with Jesse standing by her near the door.

"Better listen to the old man, kid. Nothing good is waiting for us out there," Kinth steps forward, speaking as quietly as he could.

Another loud boom shakes the building, causing the ceiling to crack with pieces of it falling from above them.

"Oh no! I'm too late!" Feeza says aloud from across the room. "He's here."

Laughing evilly, The Guardian approaches the door with his men close by. "Sounds like we are in for a treat!"

Across the room, the various other groups begin to activate their abilities and weapons in preparation for whatever was on the other side of the door. Langston finally ran behind Jesse and Talicia into the employee break room. Aldo, Enrico, and some others blocked the main entrance, using tables and anything else they could find nearby.

HAKRA

The old man stays behind, sitting at a table alone.

Chapter 26

FRONT ENTRANCE - HOSTEL

"FEEZA!" A CREATURE'S RASPY, DEEP VOICE COULD BE heard yelling out from the path in front of the hall. The sound of its voice pierces through the doors like a knife through soft butter. Growing impatient, it yells again. Only, this time, it stretches out the syllables of her name, "FEEEEEZZZZAAAA!"

The Guardian, noticing the building crumbling more, removes the tables and opens the aging door. As the door opens and creaks loudly, The Guardian looks over his shoulder and says smugly, "Better come out here, pretty lady. Seems you have been beckoned."

Stepping outside and just in front of the entrance, The Guardian is greeted by a large creature. Several others stand to its side and behind. The large, disturbing creature wears only pants and work boots. Shirtless, its body seems to have no skin. It's as if someone or something had removed it, showing only the muscle layer of its body.

One-by-one, various members of the different groups follow behind The Guardian outside. While positioning themselves at various points, they notice that many members of their respective groups have been killed or bound together. Now, everyone is lined in a row.

Stunned groans and cries of anguish cover the area. The group notices their fellow friends, some of which have been draped across stones and the ground. Others are bound together and unconscious.

"Where is Feeza?" the creature asks, to no one in particular. The depth of its voice felt as if it crawled onto the skin of those nearby.

Pushing through the speechless bodies in front of her, Feeza makes her way to the front of the group. After scanning the hills, she says, "He sent you? I'm surprised he didn't come himself."

"Return to Ifera at once. Come peacefully and no one else will have to suffer," the creature says, stepping forward.

Feeza sighs and begins to approach the creature, who stands a few feet taller than her.

"You're not going anywhere with our friends! Release them now!" Mathias says, cracking his knuckles. Several others yell out and wave their weapons in agreeance.

Several yards behind the wall of creatures, the group of allies are bound together. Most of them are wounded. Their coughs and groans echo across the hilly land.

Making his way outside, Kinth gradually moves toward the front with his support behind him. After quickly glancing at the group of creatures in his view, as well as the fallen bodies nearby, he realizes that those with him may not be a match for what stands before them. The beasts at Delrusia Island were primitive and clumsy. Something about the creatures standing before him now seem calculated and advanced.

Kinth also couldn't trust that his brother would put their differences aside to rally together, should there be a fight.

"Damn, it's a lot of them," Aldo says, leaning in toward Kinth to whisper. "And who is the skinny, loud mouth speaking for everybody?"

"That's Mathias of Fetela. His father and my father were close," Kinth replies. "He is a skilled warrior. I'm not sure how he got here, but I'm glad that he is here."

"Shit, I hope so."

Folding his arms, Enrico narrows his vision on the odd, muscular creatures. Shaking his head subtly, he says, "I have never seen anything like them before."

One of the fallen lies just inches away from the creature's feet. She is alive but in deep anguish, moaning as she gurgles blood in her mouth. The creature, upon hearing the sound, glances at the injured woman as Feeza makes it to his side. Looking up, the creature stares deeply at Mathias. "Another word and your friends will die," it says calmly.

Someone in the group yells, "Fuck you!"

"Alright then," the creatures says after a moment. Glancing over his shoulder, he nods at another creature from his group.

This specific creature looks both to its left and its right, delivering an order with a simple stare. Then, several other creatures join in. They remove technologically advanced bows from their backs. These bows use see-through arrows with tracking abilities.

Laughing, Aldo says, "Aww, look, Kinth. They brought bows and arrows to a much, much larger fight."

Kinth, as well as several others, chuckle.

With one swift motion, the creatures activate their bows. After one quick burst of a high-pitched sound, several arrows are launched through the air - directed at everyone standing in front of the hostel.

"DUCK!" yells Jack. But his cry is too late. Arrows are released only seconds afterwards.

The special arrows soar through the air from various directions, following those who tried to run and piercing their bodies. Almost everyone is hit, except for those fortunate enough to find cover. Some of the others were brave enough to storm toward the line of creatures, fighting with every morsel of strength they have.

The muscular creature nodded again, but this time towards the hills. He commands another group of archers to load more arrows, but these arrows were connected together through neuro-netting. Aiming high, these archers launch from their position. Arrows fall at various locations around those who still remained, enclosing them in one big trap.

The Guardian, however, managed to avoid the trap and angrily ran toward the hill. "What are you doing?! You have my men in the trap with the others! This is not what we had agreed!"

Huffing, the creature shoves The Guardian out of the way, using so much force that The Guardian slides several feet across the ground. The odd, muscular specimen then pulls a small device from its pocket, activating it. After momentarily waiting for the device to do something, the creature presses a button. This prompts the arrow's roping to tighten. Therefore, the trap could be grabbed and tied at four ends. After self-tightening and tying, individual roping attaches itself to the arms and legs of everyone inside. Pressing another button, the creature sends an electric shock through the roping that knocks everyone out.

As several creatures grab the rope from opposite ends, others position themselves in the middle. They carry the bodies over the hills. The leader of the group, inspecting the rope as well as the bodies, looks back once more at the area around the hostel. Stopping, he stares for a moment. He ensures that he didn't miss anything. As he scans the area, his eyes become fixed at the peak of a hill toward the rear of the hostel. He notices a quick glimmer of light at this peak. Looking over his shoulder, he grunts an order to some others in his group. Three other creatures begin to make their way around the side of the hill.

On the other side of the hostel, Langston, Jesse, and Talicia watch the activity from behind thick brush while at the peak of a hill. The three had successfully made their way through the rear secret exit of the hostel. They were making their way over the hills before they heard the commotion taking place in front of the venue.

"I wish we could help them," Jesse says. "We can't just leave them."

Kneeling on one knee to duck within the brush, Langston moves some of the foliage from his face. "Yeah, but it's too many of them. I'm not sure what we can do."

Talicia is practically connected to Langston's back, crouching behind him as much as she can to get her own view of what was happening. Her nervousness causes her leg to shake anxiously, which further causes her large earrings to move around. This movement catches a bit of the light from the sky, reflecting it briefly across the area.

Squinting a bit, Jesse doesn't take his eyes off the line of creatures as they walk away. "Mr. Langston, look!"

Langston repositions himself to change his vantage point, noticing that a group of creatures were walking in a different direction. After watching them for a moment, the creatures disappear behind some hills.

"Where are the other ones going?" Jesse adds, inquisitively. He and the others sit quietly for what seemed like forever. They continue watching to see whether or not the creatures would reappear again.

Gravel begins to bounce across the ground because of rumbling footsteps getting louder. The creatures, who had disappeared behind the hills, signaled others within their group that had already been positioned behind the hostel. After getting the alert, this separate group of creatures moved toward the hill to search the area.

Feeling the rumbling beneath her feet, Talicia peaks her head out from the brush. Quickly she is grabbed from behind and turned around briskly. "Langston! Look out!" She screams, just before she is grabbed by the throat and lifted into the air.

Turning around aggressively, Langston darts toward Talicia and jumps on the beast from behind. "Jesse, run!" he says while he pounds on the head of the creature with all his might. "Go! Now!"

With little effort, the creature slings Langston to the ground. He places one of its feet on Langston's chest to keep him from moving. Startled by this, Jesse quickly changes the color of his body to blend in with the brush completely. The only remnants of him being present are the slight movements of the brush as he runs back toward the hostel.

"Find the kid!" one of the other creatures shouts aggressively. "And be quick about it. So that we don't keep Hakra waiting any longer." Yanking at the arms of Langston and Talicia, he takes them to rejoin the larger group of captives over the hills.

As the various creatures dissect the area, Jesse uses this time wisely. He makes his way down the hill, at times stumbling on the lumpy ground to the rear entry of the hostel.

At this point, the environment inside of the hostel is quiet. Most of the patrons had either left before the commotion, during, or succumbed to the violent visitors thereafter. Winston is still sitting at a corner table, sipping the contents of a random cup slowly. Then, he hears the sounds of footsteps and then a door opening.

Entering the employee break area first and then the kitchen, Jesse clumsily knocks over various things such as a trash can and a cart containing used dishes. Meanwhile, he tries to get to the main hall. His actions alert the old man, who had been resting his eyes while he drank.

"Jesse! What are you doing back here?" Winston says, shifting his body around to face him. "You and the others were supposed to get out of here!"

Out of breath, Jesse replies, "I – I know, but those big guys surprised us from behind. They got Mr. Langston and his friend. Everyone who came out the front entrance is being taken away, too."

"Oh dear."

"And they said something about not keeping someone waiting. A weird name." Sliding onto to a seat, Jesse rests his head on his hand wearily.

"Hakra," the old man says, coldly. He scratches his beard, with a frown developing on his face.

"Yes! That's it!"

Frustratingly, Winston rears back in his chair. He lets his head fall in despair. "I thought I would never hear that name again."

"Who is he?"

"Well, my young friend, he was a person with a lot of opinions. He and I disagreed with a lot of things while we served on the counsel. I think I told you about the counsel, yes? Or maybe that was Langston. Anyway, there were several of us. We would meet with the original Guardian, assisting and advising him on various things. Mostly, we assisted him on how to best lead the city that we loved. Just imagine you and your friends, and one of you had to be the leader. That person would ask you for help from time to time."

Jesse lays his head down on his arms on the table, listening attentively.

"But eventually, just like Franklin, Hakra became indifferent with our ways to run the city. He and Franklin became, uh, good friends because of their similar opinions. Ultimately, Hakra left the city. I thought that was the end of his name. Here I thought it was just Franklin that was causing all of this unrest, but it seems he has had help. I guess I have been in denial."

"So what are we going to do?" Jesse asks. "Are we going after them?"

Looking down the table, Winston grabs a plate of food and slides it in front of the two of them. He fingers at the leftovers of bread, chunks of meat and rice to locate the best portions. "Eat. It looks like it's . . . just us two now. Get your fill and then we'll leave to do what we can."

"But do you know where we need to go?"

Leaning forward and resting his hand on Jesse's forearm, Winston replies with a smile, "Well . . . we will trust our instincts, just as we have always had to do."

Chapter 27

THE LAB – IFERA HOSPITAL

A DEEP RUMBLING AND REPETITIVE SOUND RESONATES against Kinth's ears, reminding him of when he was much younger. He often heard his father vacuum the living room floor assertively from down the hall. It was a muffled and dull sound because of the walls, but still, it was loud enough to alert Kinth after he had been asleep.

Blinking his eyes slowly, Kinth awakens. He finds himself unable to move. Squirming a little, he notices that his arms are strapped down tightly. Wires are connected to various points of his body, while more tubing is connected to various points of his head. Slowly he turns to look to his left and then to his right, but he's unable to see much.

What he can see just in front of him is Feeza. She is strapped to a chair with her back turned to him, her head dangling to the side. She was either dead or unconscious. In front of her are some of the others, all inside similar enclosures like the one Kinth is in. Aldo who was still unconscious, was in Kinth's direct line of sight. Mathias was to Aldo's right, while random prisoners and Ekladi people were on either side.

Moving his gaze upward, Kinth notices the large tube in the center of the room that extends fully to the ceiling. His eyes follow the tube, noticing the streams and flickers of light within of it. Large wires run from it to the individual cylinders. It begins to dawn on him that the changes in the sky – the cycling of light – probably was caused by this place.

Various lab technicians are moving about the testing facility rapidly. All are pressing buttons on long, well-lit computer machinery. Tall beasts stand at various corners like statues, watching all of the movements. Seemingly, the only part of their body that moves are their eyes.

Jerking more, Kinth does his best to scan the room. He looks specifically for his Uncle Winston, Langston, and Jesse. But he cannot see part of the room. His movements cause his cylinder to shake, moving the tubes and fluids enough to catch the attention of the lab technicians.

Standing around him, Kinth watches as these technicians' converse and look at clipboards. Some write various things, pointing at Kinth and studying him as if he were a zoo animal. Others click buttons on a nearby wall, which causes changes within Kinth's cylinder. These changes cause Kinth to groan in pain, loud enough to reach the ears of almost everyone moving about the room.

Turning their heads away in unison, the group of workers' behavior causes Kinth to become curious regarding that at which they were looking. Unable to hear anything, Kinth watches the group step to either side to let someone else approach his cylinder.

A tall person, wearing dark clothing with most of his face covered, approaches the cylinder, and crosses his arms. "Well, it seems at least one of my newest subjects is awake! Thought I had a bit more time, but I guess not."

The man's words are muffled to Kinth, since he is unable to make out anything said at this point.

"Turn on the monitors, you idiots," the man continues. "My new subjects can't hear me."

Running toward the master control board, one of the lab technicians sits down quickly. They press a button just underneath the word MONITOR. A slight hum fills the room, and apparent feedback begins coming from the collection of devices.

Inside the cylinders, Kinth and the others, who have been slowly regaining consciousness, can hear anything outside of the cylinders when this button is pressed.

"Ah! That's better! Not that it matters, but it would be rude of me not to introduce myself. My name is Hakra. You _"

Storming into the room, The Guardian walks in with three of Hakra's security team behind him. Angrily, he approaches Hakra and interrupts him. "What the hell is going on? Why did you have me held up in that other room?! Like – like I am one of these guinea pigs!"

The growing argument causes Feeza to slowly awaken.

"Have a seat, Franklin," Hakra says, pulling up a chair beside Feeza.

Squinting his eyes, Kinth tries his best to figure out what is going on between Hakra and his brother. He further tries to discover how to break himself free from the enclosure. The activity in front of him is growing more intense.

"*Have a seat?* Why? Why is this –"The Guardian glances over the cylinders, noticing Kinth in the cylinder just feet away. "Wait a minute! This wasn't a part of our agreement! My family was not a part of this deal!"

HAKRA

The Guardian is grabbed by both his arms and shoved down onto the seat. Then, he is strapped down in the same fashion as Feeza who is sitting next to him.

The Guardian, growing exacerbated, shouts, "What are you doing?!"

Hakra kneels to meet The Guardian's eyes with his own. He studies his face for a moment before saying, "Franklin, I have had enough of you. You have become exhausting." Grabbing his sidearm from beneath his cloak, Hakra quickly points it at The Guardian's head and pulls the trigger. Blood from The Guardian's head splatters across Kinth's cylinder.

"Sir! Please! You can't do these types of things near the test equipment!" one of the lab technicians shouts, scrambling to clean the area.

Arrogantly, Hakra says, "Oh, its fine. It had to be done."

Although muffled, Kinth screams in anguish at the sight of his brother being murdered. He screamed so loudly, in fact, that the bass within his scream awakens everyone else in the room who had been unconscious.

Slowly regaining coherence, Feeza notices The Guardian's dead body next to her. Screaming, she jerks away so hard that she falls over onto the floor. She bangs her head against it, falling unconscious again momentarily.

Between Kinth's scream and the commotion on the lab floor, everyone is now awake and listening closely to the sounds coming through their monitors.

Standing upright, Hakra slowly holsters his sidearm. He wipes his hands as if he just completed a daunting task. Sighing heavily, he approaches Kinth's cylinder and continues his speech. "Now that I finally got that out of the way, let me continue. You are probably wondering why you are here. So, let me get right to the point. This place represents life and longevity; eternal existence. In this place, I have been working to create a way to live forever by harnessing the power from the object of which everyone was afraid. Take a look around. Please notice the advancements I have made. It took many years to accomplish, but we are close. You, as well as these others with you, are going to help me greatly."

Slowly coming to herself, Feeza replies in anguish, "Please, please, Hakra . . . no more. Please . . . not these people."

Hakra quickly walks toward Feeza, lifting her upright. "Their measly lives have purpose now. Do you not understand this?"

Feeza breathes heavily, gazing at the floor.

HAKRA

"You see . . . this place wouldn't exist without you and you and you," Hakra points at each cylinder, before returning his stare toward Kinth. "When I served on your father's counsel, I watched him put the wrong type of hope into the people. Hope that inspired them to go backwards. To return to what we once were instead of inspiring them to embrace what we could be – what we could eventually become! Greater! More resilient! Unstoppable.

"I managed to convince your brother to join me in support of my ideology. I needed his support since he had access to your father's resources. But your brother grew more annoying over time. My patience in regards to him grew thin, as you have clearly seen just a moment ago."

Taking a breather, Hakra paces around the lab floor. He glances over the shoulders of his technicians as they worked. During this moment of quiet, the lab doors open and more of Hakra's scouts walk in.

"We have a couple more to add to the others. We caught them hiding in the brush in the hills. Something is different about this one. He smells weird." The beast shoves Langston to the floor.

"Smells weird? What do you mean?" Hakra replies, walking towards Langston. Quickly he grabs Langston by his face as if Langston was a young child. Hakra stares into his eyes. Rolling up Langston's sleeves, he gazes at his skin.

Using his finger, he follows the outline of Langston's veins. His eyes widened with disbelief. "Hmm. Take this one and his friend to one of the available room's near Feeza's."

Making their way on a narrow, brush-filled path, Jesse follows behind the old man. They walk in the direction of the Ifera hospital, which sits between the mountains of Dyadika. Using his abilities to guide them again, the old man begins to slow in his pace and coughs every so often. At first, Jesse seems to be unaware of how often Winston coughs. But eventually, he takes notice.

"You okay?" Jesse asks softly.

"Yes, yes. Let's keep going."

Taking a few more unsteady steps, Winston coughs again and grabs his chest in anguish. He then plops down to the ground, leaning against one of a collection of large stones.

Breathing heavily, Winston rests his head on the stone, gazing at the sky while sweating profusely. "I – I can't go any further. But you can, my young friend. By the looks of it, you don't have much further to go. Just over those hills . . . Do you see that?" Winston points at the vague view of the top of a building which is almost hidden behind some hills.

"I can't do this without you!" Jesse replies, shaking his head.

Winston doesn't respond right away. Instead, he creates a brief pause in the conversation. The moment of silence allows for the sound of the wind, blowing the brush and soil to pass through the area. Looking around a bit, the old man lets out a sound of relief. "It's quite beautiful when you actually take the time to sit and look at it."

Looking up, Jesse nods.

"I know that you have spent most of your young life with my niece, the Madam. But it would be unwise of me to presume that she educated you on your past." Winston coughs more, his condition worsening. "Do you know why she is so fond of you?"

"Because I've been with her for so long. And I bring her stuff," Jesse replies, shrugging.

Laughing loudly, the old man rolls onto his side to regain his composure after having caused more coughing to ensue. A strange fluid begins to slowly come from one of his nostrils.

Wiping his nose subtly, the old man becomes serious. "Jesse, it appears my time is limited. So, here is the truth. Your biological mother had a hard time accepting you and your abilities when you were very small. She left you on a doorstep in the city, and you were later brought to The Guardian's mansion. After much discussion, we thought it would be best to place you in the Madam's care. We all knew you were special, but I – I knew much more about you."

"More? Like what?"

"You have other gifts. Use them . . . at that place," Winston says, pointing in the direction of the hills. "When you get there, use them!"

"Other gifts?"

Gently resting onto the ground, Winston's breathing slows. His remaining words come out garbled and slow. "Believe . . . your – yourself . . . believe."

"Wait! Wait! Wake up! Wake up!" Jesse says, shaking the old man multiple times. Standing, Jesse begins to step backwards while at a loss for words. He is too shocked to cry. Nervously he looks around, thinking that he might have alerted threats to his location by screaming out.

Releasing a slow, deep breath, Jesse starts walking toward the building just beyond the hills. A little confidence grows within him with each step he takes, and he slowly realizes he is the last hope to save his friends.

Chapter 28

THE LAB – IFERA HOSPITAL

ALL EYES OF THOSE WITHIN THE CYLINDERS CLOSELY FOLLOW Hakra, as the mystery man continues pacing the lab floor. His gaze moves quickly from the machinery to the test subjects and to his technicians, while his thoughts focus on his mission.

Walking pass a cylinder, Hakra notices Jack moving his head and eyes erratically. It appeared as if he was trying to say something.

"You, come here." Hakra says, pointing to one of his technicians before looking back at Jack. "Seems this subject has something to share. Let's take a moment to humor him; enjoy some entertainment."

Approaching the cylinder, the technician presses a few buttons. He turns a couple of dials, causing the cylinder's pressure to decrease. Air is slowly released. Then, the tubing attached to Jack's mouth is removed by a robotic arm built within the cylinder.

His head falls from the release of the mouth attachment. Jack breathes in and out deeply. "Why – why are you doing this? What do you want from us? What the hell have you done with our friends?!"

Chuckling to himself, Hakra beings to pace again. "Ohh. That's right! I wasn't finished explaining things." He walks with his hands now clasped together and behind his back, glancing at his technicians again. "Make sure that everyone can hear me."

Clicking the monitor button again, one of the technicians steps backward into the shadows upon this action being completed.

"Now . . . where were we? Oh! 'Why am I doing this?' was your question. It's simple, actually. The goal here is to live forever. The technology you see around you is helping me achieve that. What we are doing is using the best genetics of all of you to create a species of people who will never die; or at the least, live for a very, very long time. My team has been searching the hills of the Pines for years. They sought to find only the best and healthiest people in which we can use here. This also includes humans. Humans have certain antibodies of which hybrids have little. But sadly, humans have become sparse. So, I must rely on you."

Hakra then motions to another technician. He gives a non-verbal instruction to which not only this particular technician follows, but the others around him do as well. The technician takes a short step forward toward one of the control boards, flipping a switch. At this moment, a cylinder containing one of Mathias's people illuminates. Fluid begins to run through the various tubing and the air pressure increases. It moves the excess, unneeded fluids of this person up and out of the cylinder and into the master tube in the center of the lab.

Screaming in anguish, the sounds of the man's pain draw attention from everyone in the room.

Watching attentively from his cylinder, Mathias releases a muffled plea. "Nooo!"

"See. This . . . is your purpose now," Hakra says, gazing at the ceiling. "Most people ran from the object that fell. I ran towards it! I was intrigued by it. I studied it. Before the government came and removed it, I was able to take enough from it to use here."

Lying flat on the ground under bushes at the peak of the nearest hill, Jesse studies the activity around the hospital business park. Armed guards patrol the perimeters. Other creatures lurk about, both on the grounds and way out upon the hills. Sizing up the guards, Jesse realizes that he is puny compared to the security at this place. He begins to doubt what the old man said to him just before he took his last breath. But there's no one else to do what needs to be done.

He notices that the hills and mountain behind the business park are quite darker than the area around it. Except, this is not the case at the apex of the mountain. From what he can tell, the land descends at the back of the business park. It's as if it led to something that was meant to be hidden.

The size and layers of the mountain have Jesse captivated. Squinting his eyes a bit, he sees what appears to be fast-moving light traveling away from the apex of the mountain. He follows the lights with his eyes, as they enter into the sky. Then, it disperses into various directions and eventually blends in with the sky's current color.

Taking a moment to think, Jesse quickly realizes that his mission to save the others is no different than any other mission on which Madam Pearl had sent him. This time, however, he needs to find his friends instead of finding goods that the Madam could use.

Snapping out of his thoughts, he quickly begins to jog down the hill toward the front gate of the business park. With each object he passes, he changes the color of his body and clothing to blend with it; camouflaging himself. But his effort to blend in with his environment can't happen as rapid as he would like. Rather, it causes him to be seen by the frontline security at the business park.

To make matters worse, Jesse crosses a laser alert line that triggers an alarm. At the sound of the alarm, the guards begin to fire at him violently. But Jesse's swift movements and chameleon-like abilities makes him a hard target.

"Where did he go?!" shouts one of the guards.

"Just keeping firing!"

Jesse quickly runs to the side of the main entrance, running alongside the tall fence that protects the business park. He looks for any alternative entry inside. Attempting to climb the fence, a surge of electricity quickly bolts into his body. It causes him to jolt away from the barrier.

A quick yelp alerts the guards to his location. "Over here!"

Out of breath from being thrown from the fence and practically fried to death, Jesse musters up enough energy to hide himself once more. He does so just as the guards walk up to his location.

"Where did he go?" one of the guards ask nervously, moving around the grounds with purpose. He stabs his spear into the brush, spreading the long strands apart while hoping to hit anything. "He was just here!"

"Maybe he ran off. Probably one of the usual stragglers. He might be drunk off ale from that watering hole a few miles from here."

Holding his weapon tightly, one of the large commanders approaches. He wears a long coat that drags the ground a few feet behind him. He sniffs around, holding his eyes closely to the ground. "Back to your stations. He's not getting in here without us knowing."

As the commander stays behind to get one last look around, he notices the brush around this particular part of the perimeter was higher than it was supposed to be. "Hey! Get the grounds people to come chop this shit down some. It's getting too high."

Moments later, landscapers quietly come with tools and wheel-barrels to chop down the brush. Sometimes, they come close to hitting Jesse in the process. He had been laying perfectly still, holding his breath at times. As the maintenance team strategically place the chopped brush into the wheel-barrels, Jesse hops into one. He hides underneath a stack of the chopping.

After the uncomfortableness of listening to moans and groans of manual labor, Jesse could feel himself being lifted and rolled away. The landscapers move the barrels of trimmed brush down a path parallel to the business park. It leads to the rear of it, near the mountain behind the area further.

An excruciating, repulsive smell begins filling the air and causes Jesse's stomach to turn. Peeking out the small holes beneath the brush, he can see what appears to be piles of something yards away. *What is that?* he thinks.

"Alright! Unload it and let's get back to our more important matters!" someone hollers from the distance.

Unexpectedly, Jesse can feel his lower torso lift upward and aggressively. Suddenly, he begins to tumble head first beneath the brush and down a hill. Feeling as if he had been rolling endlessly, Jesse abruptly comes to a halt. He hits what he believes to be a large stone or embankment. Jesse listens carefully before peaking his head out from the brush, ensuring that whoever dumped him was gone.

Shock overcomes him. A rancid smell hits his nose, causing him to throw up almost immediately. Wiping his mouth, he climbs out of the brush and looks around. Piles of bodies are everywhere - all thrown into a large, circular ditch. Jesse's eyes widen; his mouth quivers. He had never seen anything like this in his life. His feet landed on the remains of a person almost everywhere he stepped. Large and small; young and old. Jesse's eyes began to fill with water as he continued to examine the area. It appeared to be an apparent dumping ground of those who had filled their purpose to the hospital but were no longer needed. The sight of this place was so traumatic that the color of Jesse's skin and clothing began to change almost on its own, as if someone was rapidly changing television channels.

Standing in horror, Jesse's legs grow heavy. For a moment, his mind flashes. He quickly reflects on all the runs he made for Madam Pearl while in her care. The brief encounters, strange people, fights and getaways. *But nothing he had been through prepared him for this place,* he thought.

A weird, distorted, animal-like sound reaches his ears; along with short, deep bursts of air. Narrowing his eyes, Jesse sees large creatures that resemble scorpions. They move about the piles of remains. Dozens of them are various sizes. They hover over the bodies, using their chela's to grab and pick through dinner. They rip through their pickings, sucking up the pieces gradually and putting them into their mouths.

Scrambling to find a way out, Jesse notices a winding path that leads to a dark area. Maybe a tunnel or entrance? There are small, subtle blinking lights strategically placed on the path that seem promising. Quietly he runs toward the lights, blending in with the bodies at times to stay hidden. Once at the end of the path, he cautiously walks down the steel walkway. Jesse tip-toes to avoid alerting the large scorpion-like beasts.

Chapter 29

JESSE – IFERA HOSPITAL

AS JESSE SLOWLY MOVES DOWN THE PATH, VARIOUS sounds toward the end of the tunnel grow louder. Mechanical noises, bursts of air, and the clicking and humming of equipment, all fall upon his ears. Sometimes the sounds are loud enough to startle him. They cause him to consider turning around and saying good-bye to the idea of a solo rescue mission.

Pausing for a moment, Jesse quickly thinks about a conversation he had with Madam Pearl a while ago, before he went on a run for her. He was almost out the door of her penthouse when she called him over:

"Come here and let me take a look at ya before you go. Mmm hmm. You got everything? I'm so *proud* of you, boy. Ain't too much in this place to be proud of. All the gambling, scrambling and fighting out there. But you – you are at the top of my 'most proud of' list." Madam Pearl repositions on the couch, straightening up Jesse's loose and out-of-place clothing affectionately. "You know, I am not sure why I was chosen to look after you. My mothering skills aren't the greatest but . . . but I'm glad I was. There is something special about you. I'm talking really special. I don't know what it is. I can just feel it all the way down to my toes! Remember that when you are out there in the city . . . and *really* remember that when you go beyond those walls. Mm'kay?"

Sounds of footsteps snap Jesse out of his thoughts. The wide tunnel door makes a sound just before opening. At this moment, Jesse quickly backs up against one of the walls, blending into the darkness. Walking by are various lab workers conversing amongst themselves. Many are pushing large carts full of bodies. Noticing familiar faces in the carts, Jesse quickly covers his mouth in fear. He hopes to avoid making any sounds to alert the workers to his hiding spot.

Before the doors close, Jesse darts beyond them and goes down the tunnel. A few yards away is another set of doors, followed by a large glass window. Past the window are more workers, appearing to sort through bodies. They remove anything valuable from the lifeless test subjects before tossing the remains into various carts. Stretching his neck to see more of the room, Jesse notices steps that spiral upward. They ascend against one of the walls toward the back of the room. There is also a lift in the middle of the room, but with all the activity around, it would be unwise for him to try to get to it.

Quietly, Jesse waits for the glass door to open. Once it does, he inches his way inside. Then, Jesse gradually moves more inside by staying closer to the wall. He finally gets to the spiraling steps and begins to climb them. He grows anxious at one point, when he plants his foot too hard on one of the steps which causes the steps to squeak. Some of the lab workers pause what they were doing to look around. But then, they continue their work after confirming that they must have been hearing things.

Unsure on where to go at this point, Jesse wonders aimlessly for a moment. He listens for any clues on where his friends might be. Without warning, he hears a muffled scream that startles him. He cowers in the corner of a hallway, blending in with the dark before continuing. Just as Jesse begins to take another step, a lab worker comes around the corner and the two collide.

In shock, the lab worker doesn't know what to do. Without thinking, Jesse jumps on the worker, pummeling him until he is unconscious. The force behind Jesse's blows was as if he channeled the help of a several warriors to assist him. Stunned by his actions, Jesse's confidence skyrockets. *Where did this strength come from?* he thinks. He grabs the worker by one leg and drags him into the dark corner. Quickly Jesse removes the worker's clothing. After trying on the outfit, he realizes that it's too big for him to wear, and so, his idea of a disguise would not work. As he is trying to decide what to do, more lab personnel come down the hall. They notice the tip of one of the worker's foot slightly protruding from the darkness.

Jesse can hear the commotion of the others brewing, prompting him to blend in with the wall quickly. The group of various lab personnel storm his location, in an uproar about the unconscious and practically undressed worker lying on the floor. After reviewing the man and helping him up, the group retreats back in the direction from which they came. At this moment, Jesse realizes that this might be his last opportunity to find the others. So, he runs with the group and uses his ability to blend in with the clothing they are wearing.

Approaching a set of large doors, one of the technician's scans his hand. He walks into the main laboratory, with the others following closely behind him. "Hakra! Hakra!" one of the technicians shout.

Jesse is so stunned by the sight of the technology within the lab that he stands perfectly still for a moment. He gazes up at the lights, moving through the cylinder that extends to the apex of the room. He gazes so long that he almost misses his chance to enter the room as the doors close. Darting through the doors, a piece of his pants gets caught between them. After pulling his leg, he tears his pants slightly, but not enough to notice the cloth hit the floor.

"Hakra!" The technician shouts once more, waving to get his attention. The technician is helping to carry the man who had been attacked by Jesse.

Jolting around, Hakra grows frustrated. "Yes! Yes! What is it?"

Jesse quickly runs toward one of the large pieces of machinery, hiding behind it to get a closer look. The machine is about twice his height, with various buttons and levers. As he peaks around the device, his mouth falls open. Suddenly, he notices the bodies of people inside the smaller cylinders. Most of the faces are familiar to him but not the faces he'd hoped to find.

"Someone attacked him!"

"Someone who?" Hakra asks.

"I don't know. We found him unconscious a few corridors away."

HAKRA

Walking briskly to a monitor on the wall, Hakra presses the talk button frustratingly. "Front Gate," he says before taking his finger off of the button.

"Yes," a brute voice responds strongly.

Leaning his head further into the monitor to ensure he is heard, Hakra continues insistently, "What is going on out there?"

"Nothing, sir. Drunken stragglers, we believe. But we handled it. They're gone."

Annoyed, Hakra replies, "Are you certain?"

"Yes."

Kinth, Aldo, Enrico and Jack are all conscious at this point. All are watching and studying what's going on in the room as best as they could from their individual vantage points.

Pausing for a moment, Hakra looks at the technicians closely. It was as if he suspected them of causing the same commotion they were reporting. Then, he nods to two large creatures positioned against the wall. Both immediately walk toward the main doors. One of the creatures walks briskly through the doors, but the other, after unconsciously looking down at the floor, notices the small piece of clothing on the floor.

Jesse uses this time wisely as Hakra and his workers investigate the incident he caused. Moving around the room's perimeter while scanning each cylinder, he notices Kinth and the other familiar faces from his travels. Darting across the room, Jesse moves too quickly for his abilities to keep up. He nearly gives away his position as a result. He slides beneath the control board of one of the long computers just in front of Kinth's cylinder.

Stopping suddenly, the creature who found the piece of clothing turns around sharply and shouts, "AN INTRUDER IS IN THE ROOM!" Quickly he walks toward a button that sits inside a glass housing. He lifts the small door and slams his hand on the button. All the doors within the room make a sound before closing. Most of the machinery quiets to a sleep state.

"FIND THEM!" Hakra yells in response.

At this moment, Jesse reveals himself under the computer. He waves his hand so that Kinth can see that he is there.

Growing weaker, it takes a couple moments for Kinth to notice Jesse is trying to get his attention. An unexpected, muffled scream from one of the people next to Kinth alerts and causes him to focus. Once he sees Jesse, Kinth believes he is at first hallucinating. He shakes his head in an effort to snap out of what he believes is his mind playing tricks on him.

The muffled screams from the person next to Kinth continues, prompting Jesse to hold his finger over his mouth in his attempt to quiet them. Unconsciously, Jesse makes a *Shh* sound. But realizing how foolish it was, he regrets it soon after.

"What's that?" One of the lab workers responds to the strange sound, walking toward the area. "It sounds like it came from over here."

Kinth's eyes follow the worker. The medium-sized creature wears tiny, round glasses and walks in front of where Jesse is hiding. Jesse scoots back more, practically smashing himself into the wall of the base of the large computer; his body colors flickering.

Oh no, he thinks.

Inspecting the area, the worker does everything but kneel and peek under the computer control board. Before he can think of this, Kinth screams and moves his body to draw attention to himself. He shakes himself and moves his body crazily, as much as he can since he is strapped down.

"What is happening to him?" Hakra speaks quietly from across the room.

"I don't know, sir. I have never seen this behavior before."

"Maybe the alarm did something to the power," the creature who sounded the alarm says.

"That's not possible. All of the cylinders are on a separate grid. Leave the thinking to us!"

As the group of workers brainstorm what they believe could be happening to Kinth, Jesse calms down enough in order to blend in with the color of the flooring in the lab. He then quietly crawls from under the computer control board and stands near it, examining the various buttons and levers. Unsure on what button to push to free his friends, Jesse presses each one to which he is drawn. He presses the buttons individually, while watching the room to see what each one does thereafter.

The first button doesn't seem to do anything that he can see, nor the second button. The third one he presses causes another computer to beep and boot up, making subtle noises and humming. This computer's action activates some of the lights on the individual cylinders, alerting the workers.

"LOOK! LOOK AT THE LIGHTS! SOMEONE IS CONTROLLING THE EQUIPMENT! THEY ARE IN HERE! THEY MUST HAVE ABILITIES!"

Short on time, Jesse is startled by the person's shouting. So, he begins to press all of the buttons randomly. One of the buttons causes the air inside of the cylinder to decrease excessively. The people inside these cylinders begin to breathe heavily, and their eyes widen with worry. Kinth continues his performance but keeps his gaze on Jesse's actions.

His stomach tightens. Jesse feels as though he is about to explode with the amount of anxiety and adrenaline flowing through his body. At this moment, it seems like the time slowed. He focused his eyes on one particular button that he hadn't pressed yet. Reaching for it slowly, he closes his eyes with hopes that this button was the right choice. Pressing it firmly, a loud buzzer goes off in the room, just before the sound of a burst of air.

"OH NO!" one of the workers scream. "THEY HAVE RELEASED THE SUBJECTS!"

Realizing that they have been freed, slowly the various test subjects exit their cylinders. Some fall from their anguish. Others move too quickly, realizing that their energy has been weakened. But one of the Ekladi people were strong enough to use the air from the cylinders. It created a burst of wind within the room, moving it strongly around to knock over most of the workers standing nearby.

Sliding up slowly, the door to Kinth's cylinder makes a subtle opening sound. It's loud enough to alert some of the workers nearby. Kinth's size alone is enough to make these workers pause in their position. A sense of fearful wonder fills their being that they hadn't felt until this moment.

"THE BIG ONE IS LOOSE!" says one of the workers.

Kinth slowly pulls the wires and tubing from his body, breathing heavily.

Distraught by the activity, Hakra darts for the exit while commanding his team, "HANDLE THIS! I WILL RETURN!"

Although they are bulky, intimidating beings, the lab-security creatures are slightly smaller. Even in Kinth's tormented state, they are still weaker than him. Two of them rush Kinth without thinking, pummeling him before he has the chance to completely step out of his cylinder. It causes Kinth to fall on the floor not too far away from where his dead brother lies.

With tears growing in his eyes, Kinth lies flat for a moment. He stares in agony at his fallen sibling. The anger inside him grows, but he doesn't move. Instead, he takes every blow from Hakra's security as if he feels nothing at all. Kinth is frozen within his emotions for a moment. But nearby, Mathias has freed himself, alongside Aldo and Enrico.

"KINTH!" Aldo screams, noticing Hakra running away. "SNAP OUT OF IT!"

The fight for freedom ensues around the room. Mathias and Enrico fend off some of the lab creatures on one side of the platform. Meanwhile, the Ekladi people join together to tackle those on the other side. Most of them are still in a bit of a daze from the testing that endured. But thankfully, Jesse freed them just in time.

Another alarm rings just as the doors close behind Hakra. Seconds later, more creatures from his security team storm the lab.

With his agony mutating into anger, Kinth fights his way up onto one knee. He blocks as many blows as he could. Briefly, he thinks about his father and their last moments at the island. This thought sends a wave of mixed emotions and adrenaline through his body. It causes him to swiftly turn to perform a leg sweep, knocking the creatures from off their feet.

After the creatures fall onto their backs, Aldo leaps into the air over Kinth. He lands on one creature with his knee, crushing its skull. Then, he grabs a machete from another. He incapacitates the other creature with one pierce of the machete into the creature's chest.

"DOES ANYONE SEE LANGSTON OR MY UNCLE?" Kinth cries out while simultaneously fending off the various beasts who charge in his direction.

Ducking and rolling, Jesse avoids an attack and runs up to Kinth's side. "I know Mr. Langston is here. I saw them grab him and his friend. But Mr. Winston . . . " Jesse shakes his head slowly.

Kinth's eyes become full of anger.

The battle within the lab continues around them, with most creatures debilitated, and the lab scientists held at gunpoint.

"Please! Stop!" screams one of the lab workers. "I know who you are looking for! I can help all of you get out of here!"

Approaching the small woman slowly, Kinth crouches down in order to be at eye level with the woman. "Start talking."

"Okay, okay."

Chapter 30

THE LAST STAND – IFERA HOSPITAL

GROGGILY AWAKENING, LANGSTON BLINKS HIS EYES slowly, examining the empty room. From the looks of it, the room was once an office. It had a desk in one corner with the drawers slightly opened, while old cabinets were positioned adjacently. Folders containing thick stacks of paper were stacked almost to the ceiling near his feet.

Langston's head is pounding. Obviously, he was knocked unconscious at some point during the journey to this room. Lying on the floor on his side, his hands are tied behind his back. Behind him is Talicia, positioned upright, but she's leaning against a wall still asleep. Her hands are tied in the same fashion.

"Talicia! Talicia!" Langston whispers assertively. "Wake up!"

At this moment, Hakra bursts into the room with one of his large guards. It's the guard that originally captured everyone at the hostel.

"Good. You are awake," Hakra says, moving about the room purposely. There is another door in the room, which appears to lead to the one next to it. Hakra bolts in, taking something from this room before returning. "Grab these two and let's go. Quickly!"

Back in the lab, the small lab worker gathers her composure as best as she can. Evil stares bear down on her. She looks over the faces of the previously detained test subjects, scanning their weary and anguished expressions.

"Talk, old woman!" someone says from the group.

Jack steps forward from behind someone. "Please," he says softly.

The small woman leans forward, resting her elbows on her knees and catching her breath. "The offices in the front of the hospital . . . that's where most of us sleep. Hakra converted most of these rooms into living quarters. We have our own rooms there. That's where you will find the man and woman you are looking for. Take any elevator to the main lobby."

"That's probably where he is off to, Kinth. We gotta go, now!" Aldo chimes in.

For some reason, Kinth has many questions. So, he couldn't pull himself from the room. He kneels down on one knee in front of the woman. "What is this place?"

Aldo shouts again, "KINTH! WE NEED TO GO!" Running off, most of the others follow behind him in a hurry.

"Death. Leave now and find him. Stop him if you want to end it," the woman responds coldly.

Backing away slowly, Kinth scans the room one last time. He frowns at the sight of machinery, tubing, and wires; lights and the smell of chemicals, before turning away and running to meet with the others. On his way out, Kinth grabs a few weapons from the fallen security. He bolts down the hall. Then, he moves around a couple of corners before getting to an elevator. After pressing the button a few times, he impatiently takes the stairs, leaping over a bunch at a time to get to the main floor.

As Kinth enters the hallway leading to the hospital's main entrance, he notices that everyone from the lab are cowering behind desks, walls, and corners.

"KINTH! TAKE COVER!" someone screams.

Unaware of what is taking place, Kinth takes a couple more steps before the sound of a shot rings throughout the area. A burst of wind grazes Kinth on his cheek, quickly alerting him that someone was shooting into the building. Dropping down quickly, Kinth rolls over to an adjacent wall near Jack.

"Is that him?" Kinth asks.

"Yes, from what we can tell. Looks like he has some more people up there."

Hakra stands near a group of creatures on a hill yards away, overlooking the creatures from the front of the main gate. One has a long, glowing, sniper rifle. When the rifle locks on a target, it automatically fires. On the other side of Hakra are Langston and Talicia, on their knees with weapons positioned by their heads.

"Follow us if you will, and your friends will die!" Hakra shouts, his voice seemingly carried by the wind as it bounces off the hills.

"You won't get far," Langston says quietly. "My friends are going to get to you in one way or another."

Back down the hill and in the lobby, Mathias shakes his head. "He's bluffing."

"How do you figure?" replies Aldo, slowly leaning to get another look out the lobby windows.

Rubbing the side of his face slowly, Kinth listens to the theory quietly.

"Why would he keep them alive – separately at that - if he is so willing to kill them?" Mathias responds quickly, repositioning himself where his arm comes into the view of the sniper.

More bullets fly through the room, hitting the walls nearby.

"Shit! We can't just storm out there without a plan," Enrico chimes in after taking cover. "What are we going to do?"

Sticking his head out quickly to scan the business park in front of the hospital, Kinth clears his throat. "We just need to block their view long enough to get closer," he says before turning toward some of the Ekladi people nearby. ". . . Can y'all help us with that?"

Without saying anything, the spokesman for the Ekladi group nods. One by one, each member of the group moves closer to the main doors of the hospital and spreads out horizontally.

"On my count . . . as soon as they do their thing, we haul ass to that front gate," Kinth speaks emphatically, making eye contact with everyone else in the lobby. "Keep your head low and do whatever you need to survive."

After closing their eyes, the Ekladi people begin to move their hands slowly in a melodic motion. They lift and move the sand and foliage within the business park to their liking. Using his fingers while also whispering, Kinth counts slowly to three. He watches a natural shield of debris form in front of the building.

"Let's go!" Kinth whispers, before darting out of the main entrance of the hospital. In a zig-zag motion, he moves quickly across the grounds behind the shield. At times, he hides behind the columns that line what used to be a sidewalk.

"Sir, it appears that they are coming this way," says one of Hakra's men. "What – what is that cloud forming?"

Taking a step backwards, Hakra responds, "It doesn't matter! FIRE!"

Amongst other mechanical noises from weaponry, sounds of rapid gunfire echo from off of the hills, with bullets piercing through the shield that the Ekladi people created. It kills some of them immediately. But Kinth does not stop. Instead, he continues toward the hills as bullets graze his arms. His determination motivates many of the others, prompting them to put more energy into their abilities to help them get closer to the hills.

"KINTH! WHAT ARE YOU DOING?!" screams Aldo.

Without breaking his concentration, Kinth replies, "It will take them a few seconds to reload. We are faster than this!"

On the hill, Hakra's men look down the sight of their barrels in awe at the large man seemingly walking through their bullets unscathed. "They aren't stopping, sir! What do we do?"

"WITHDRAW!" Hakra yells, before attempting to climb the next hill. Two of his largest beasts are nearby. One carries Langston, while the other carries Talicia.

Some of the Ekladi people try to subdue Hakra by shaking and moving the ground. But at every attempt, Hakra and his goons leap and maneuver themselves to escape their traps. As the three closes in on the peak of the hill, the ground rumbles much harder than moments before. It causes Hakra to turn around and look at the Ekladi people in amazement. What was causing the ground to rumble with such force?

But the Ekladi people, along with Kinth and the others, were no longer using their abilities. They were too busy in pursuit, and momentarily wondering the same thing.

The rumbling causes the ground to shake so much that the stones begin to break apart from the hills. They rapidly roll down the sides of the hills. The sky glows just before a loud cluster of deep sounds reminiscent of thunder, echoing from off of the hills.

What have they done? Hakra thinks to himself, just before the force that caused the sounds reaches the area in which he stands. It throws him and his men several feet. Hitting his head harshly on the ground, it takes him a moment to come to himself. Once he does, he gazes over the tip of his toes. He notices that the sky's glow has heightened. He follows the glow downward, which seems like a string of fire hanging from the sky. It connects to the top of the buildings within the business park. He realizes that his testing facility exploded and was up in flames.

"NOOO! WHAT DID THEY DO?!" Hakra screams, jumping to his feet. He attempts to run back toward the buildings, only to see Kinth and the others closing in on his location. Anxiously he tries to continue the same route over the hills. But then, he feels the ground rumbling more beneath his feet. Looking back at the buildings once more, Hakra then gazes at the ground before he engages his men with a confused expression. Baffled as well, his men respond with a shrug.

Over one of the shoulders of his men, Hakra notices the appearance of a new person. He was neither someone he recognized from his labs, nor from the brief battle that took place. He also wasn't any of the test subjects Hakra encountered. This person didn't appear to be a creature or a hybrid or any true threat at all. Except, there appeared to be melee weapons and side arms in his possession. But without warning, another person takes a step to be beside this stranger, and then one more. People continued to appear until the hill before him was completely blocked with a wall of unfamiliar faces.

Out of nowhere, a voice hollers out from behind the wall of people, "Now, where you think you goin'?! Hmm?!"

Stopping in his tracks, Kinth recognizes the voice without hesitation. It was a voice he had heard for most of his life: his sister. Madam Pearl took a few more steps, standing between the large group of people. Miles followed her at one side and Kira to another. People riding the backs of various creatures rise into the air behind them.

Although Kinth is just feet away from Hakra, the sight of his sister brings an odd feeling of relief and amazement to him, causing him to freeze in place.

"MADAM PEARL!" Jesse yells ecstatically, before sprinting up the hill.

Langston uses this time wisely, pulling Talicia by the hands as best as he can. His hands are still tied as well, but he moves quickly up the hill as well.

"Oh my goodness! I thought I lost you forever!" Madam Pearl says, kneeling down while extending her arms.

Jesse falls into her grasp as if she was a warm blanket. He squeezes her so much that he blends in with the color scheme of her clothing for a moment.

"I never thought I would be saying this . . .," Langston speaks sluggishly, ". . . but I am happy to see you."

Without saying a word, Madam Pearl winks at him.

"Miss me, kid?" Miles says jokingly.

With a tear forming in his eye, Jesse looks at Miles and then at Kira, smiling.

Gently pushing Jesse behind her, Madam Pearl says, "Let momma handle this. You step back."

Confidently, Aldo and Enrico, and Jack and Mathias, come to Kinth's side. They close the gap, which appeared to be a large circle that had formed around Hakra and the remainder of his goons. Intensely, the uneasiness increases. Hakra is in shock at the sight of the people. He was grossly outnumbered.

Unsure on what to do next, Hakra keeps one hand on his holstered weapon. All the while, his eyes scan the hills.

Stepping forward, Madam Pearl reaches into her brassiere to pull out the folded paperwork she had retrieved. Unfolding it gradually, she clears her throat before speaking. "You must be . . . uh, Hakra, correct? It took me a bit to figure out what all this was in these papers. I'm not even sure I understand it all. But one thing was very clear to me. Apparently, you didn't care too much for my daddy or his ideas, and my daddy knew it. He had some serious plans, and he knew you had plans of your own, too."

"YOU KNOW NOTHING!" Hakra interjects, evilly.

"Oh, but I do! You see, these fine people around you represent the people of Uhmandra. People that my daddy wanted to protect. But people you have apparently been trying to find to fulfil your sick, twisted fantasies. Once I figured out what I needed, I went and got the brightest and the best from Uhmandra. I asked them to help me find my Jesse and my . . . wait a minute - where is Franklin?"

Sighing heavily, Kinth's head falls before he shakes it slowly. He stares sorrowfully at his sister.

"And Uncle?"

Kinth's gaze stays the same.

Jesse looks up at Pearl sorrowfully and says, "I had to leave him in the hills."

Covering her eyes with one of her hands for a moment, Madam Pearl shakes her head slowly in disbelief. With fury in her eyes, she screams at the top of her lungs, "GET HIM!"

Storming Hakra's location, the circle gets smaller. Kinth becomes the closest person to him. Hakra's men do their best to fend off some of their attackers, but there were too many. As if ants storming a pile of food on the ground, Hakra's men become completely covered by several people - both from Pearl's group and from Kinth's.

Calculating his odds frantically, Hakra falls to one knee. He curls himself inward tightly in a deep thought position. After straining for a few seconds and growling at times, he begins to glow as some people reach the hymn of his garments. Within a tenth of a second, Hakra disappears. He leaves only charred remains of where he had been crouching. Soil and rock scatter through the air, hitting those around and knocking them from off their feet when they attempted to grab him.

Smoke and the scent of burning soil are the only remains of the evil man that stood before them.

"Where did he go?" Jack says inquisitively, pacing the area.

Kneeling down by the charred soil, Kinth rubs his hands across the ground. Grabbing some of the soil and smelling it, he says, "Looks like he is long gone from here."

"Did he kill himself?" Aldo asks.

Shuffling her way closer to her brother, Madam Pearl says, "Does it matter? We need to go."

"What if he comes back?" Jesse asks, following behind Pearl closely.

Looking over his shoulder at the facilities up in flames, Kinth says, "He won't be back."

Sitting on a stone, Langston examines the landscape and the hospital. Then, he looks at the faces from Uhmandra. He recognized some, but others he'd never met until this moment.

"It's over," Talicia says quietly. "We can go home now."

"Of all the people to save the day, I would have never guessed it would be her," Langston says.

Noticing the two conversing, Madam Pearl walks over to Langston and extends her hand. "Here. I think these papers will serve you better than if I held on to them."

"What are these?" Langston says, fingering through the papers softly.

"Just read through them on your way home. You will understand."

Kinth, Aldo and the others walk up to listen.

Sighing, Langston says, "And what will you do? What will all you do?"

"Our father had a plan for a civil society. So, we will return to Hock to repair the damages that our brother created," Kinth says, before looking over at Pearl and grabbing her hand. "With our new Guardian leading us."

"YOU'RE GOING TO RUN THE CITY?!" Jesse exclaims, looking up at Pearl.

"Somethin' like that, baby boy. With the help of everyone here, and the agreement of peace between us. Are we all in agreement?"

Stepping forward, Jack says assertively, "Agreed."

"Agreed," Enrico says.

"Agreed," replies Aldo, patting Kinth on the shoulder.

"We agree to peace," Kira says, squeezing her mother affectionately.

Mathias replies, "Fetela is at your disposal."

Cheers of the new found peace cover the land.

"Go now. Return to your homes. Spread the news. We will meet again after some much needed rest," Kinth says.

Nodding, Madam Pearl chimes in, "If that ain't the damn truth."

"Cheers to the young man that saved us all!"

Several with the group lift Jesse into the air, tossing him around as they shout in victory.

As the group slowly disperses, Langston walks over to Kinth and Pearl. "Not to dampened the mood, but how do we explain what happened here? What if Hakra returns?" he asks quietly.

"We will figure it out, and we will be ready for him if that happens."

THE END

If you enjoyed HAKRA, here are other works by C. Schmidt:

Available at **Amazon** and other book retailers!

Lightning Source UK Ltd.
Milton Keynes UK
UKHW040703300622
405186UK00001B/161